Jess Carter
and the Oil Boat

Titles from Geoffrey Lewis:

Flashback
ISBN 978-0-9545624-0-3

Strangers
ISBN 978-0-9545624-1-0

Winter's Tale
ISBN 978-0-9545624-2-7

Cycle
ISBN 978-0-9545624-3-4

Starlight
ISBN 978-0-9545624-5-8

A Boy Off The Bank
ISBN 978-0-9545624-6-5

A Girl At The Tiller
ISBN 978-0-9545624-7-2

The New Number One
ISBN 978-0-9545624-8-9

L-Plate Boating
ISBN 978-0-9564536-0-0

Jess Carter
and the Oil Boat

Geoffrey Lewis

SGM
Publishing

ISBN 978-0-9564536-1-7

Printed and bound in the UK by
CPI Anthony Rowe, Chippenham SN14 6LH

First published in Great Britain in 2010 by

SGM Publishing
47 Silicon Court, Shenley Lodge, Milton Keynes, Bucks MK5 7DJ
info@sgmpublishing.co.uk
www.sgmpublishing.co.uk

As my first attempt at a story for younger readers, it is only appropriate to dedicate this book to a young man who came into my life a few years ago and changed it in ways I could never have imagined:

for Gabriel.

About The Author

Geoffrey Lewis was born in Oxford, in 1947. Educated at the City's High School, and Hatfield University (then a polytechnic),

he has since followed a varied career, including spells as a research chemist, security guard, and professional photographer. After many years in the motor trade, and eight years as the owner and captain of a canal-based passenger boat, he is now semi-retired and concentrating upon writing.

After a childhood spent close to the Oxford Canal, his love of the waterways led him to live aboard a narrowboat on the Grand Union Canal for sixteen years. Now back on dry land, he lives in Milton Keynes, within easy reach of the

The author, Geoffrey Lewis, on the *Nutfield*

towpath, and recently took on the duties of Captain on the historic pair – *Nutfield* and *Raymond* – which are to be seen at many waterways events throughout the year.

Photographer, bell-ringer, and American car enthusiast, he is currently engaged upon a number of writing projects including more stories set in the working days of England's canals.

Acknowledgements

As always with my canal stories, I have relied heavily upon that accumulated sump of knowledge which I have been lucky enough to soak up over the years from my friends and acquaintances among the boating people of today and yesterday, and it is difficult to offer anything other than a broad and unspecific 'thank you' to them all. But in the case of *Jess Carter*, I must acknowledge a great debt both to the Boat Museum Society and to their member Cath Turpin:

The BMS are the owners of the restored Clayton's horse-boat 'Gifford', and the opportunity to examine and photograph that boat during a visit to the museum at Ellesmere Port was of enormous value to me in developing this story. And Cath, although she will firmly deny it, is probably the leading expert on the history, trade and traffics of Thomas Clayton (Oldbury) Ltd. She was kind enough to both advise me during the writing, and then to read a draft of my story, and pick me up on quite a number of inaccuracies!

Other sources have been invaluable in preparing this story, too – the excellent article by Alan Faulkner about Claytons in the Spring 2006 edition of 'Narrowboat' magazine, and a fascinating book written by an ex-Claytons boatman: 'Cockerill's in the Cut' by John Blun. I have been lucky enough to meet John on a number of occasions, and chatting with him has helped me to get something of the 'feel' of the Stanlow traffic.

And a very special thank you must go to young Mac Lannaman, who appears in the role of Jesse on the front cover. It was at a boating event during the latter stages of writing this book that I was astonished to see walking around a boy who was the perfect living embodiment of my mental vision of Jesse Carter, and my gratitude goes to him and his family for agreeing that he would pose for the picture. The boat, by the way, is the Raymond, a restored wooden butty built, as was the Gifford, on Nurser's dock in Braunston, and my thanks go also to the Friends of Raymond for allowing me to 'borrow' their boat.

Chapter One

Six o'clock in the morning. The cold grey light of dawn was spreading its drab luminescence around the scene, keeping at bay any colour that might have intruded into the surroundings; a chill, dank mist swirled around the parapets of the bridge, curled like rising steam over the angled steel girders which spanned the canal as the early trains clanked and groaned their way across. Of human life, nothing was to be seen – the world could as well have been a place of mechanical monsters, of iron beasts breathing smoke and flame as they rose to their day's enigmatic pursuits.

In truth, the canals of the Black Country were places ignored, even avoided, by the human population. Hidden tracts of still, black water which passed unseen beneath bridges or behind factories, their oily surface gleaming secretly under the perpetual blanket of smoke and soot which gave the region its name, all but unknown to the men, women and children of Birmingham, Wolverhampton, Dudley, all the towns of England's industrial heartland.

Beneath the bridge, a huddled shape stirred, shifted itself into a marginally more comfortable position, and settled again. Another coal train rattled and clattered overhead, the grimy steam engine snorting and straining, and the shape stirred again, annoyance clear in the abruptness of its movement. The train passed, and only the distant rumble and murmur of the wakening town disturbed the relative quiet. But a new sound intruded – faint but clear through the cold morning air: C-lop, C-lop, C-lop, C-lop, C-lop... At first barely heard, but slowly growing more distinct, as slowly getting closer, closer... Bleary eyes peered into the gloom, the brow over them furrowed in curiosity as well as despair. A big dark shadow, head held high; a smaller shadow, walking at its haunches...

The horse gave a sudden snort as the bundle on the towpath moved again, almost under its front hooves, and stepped abruptly sideways.

'OW! Prince! You stupid 'orse, yeh stood on me foot!' The smaller shadow was hopping on one foot, holding the other in its hands.

'Wha's oop, Rosie? Whoy've yeh stopped?' A boy's voice called from somewhere in the mist to the little girl; she shouted back:

'It's Prince – 'e went soideways 'n stood on me toe!'

'Whoy'd 'e do that?'

'Oi dunno!' The small shadow took a step forward, peering into the darkness under the bridge as another train rumbled over her head: 'There's summat 'ere, Luke – a poile of ol' rags or summat!'

'Anythin' useful?' She took another step forward, reaching up to the horse's bridle as she did so; and then leapt back again as the bundle rolled over and sat up:

'OH! It's aloive, Luke! It's an ol' tramp!'

'I'm not a bleedin' tramp, I'm just a kid!' The bundle spoke as the distant boy's voice came out of the mist again: 'Joost get the 'orse past 'im 'let's get on!'

''Old on, Luke – it's a boy!'

'Never moind 'im, 'e's no concern o' our'n, we've got a job ter do. Joost get on, will yeh!'

'Not so fast Luke – it moight be a boatee kid. Row oos ter the soide, Oi'll tek a look.' A woman's voice, overriding her son. A faint splashing of water, and the dim bulk of a long narrow boat swung gradually against the bank. A stout shape, clad in long skirts with a dark red beret on her head, jumped the last few feet onto the towpath and hurried forward. The boatwoman stopped beside the little girl and bent down to look at the dishevelled figure still sitting with its back against the bridge abutment. Her brown eyes crinkled into a smile as wide dark ones looked up into them out of a face the colour of milk chocolate:

'What're yeh doin' 'ere, lad? 'Oo are yeh, what's yer name?' The deep eyes narrowed in suspicion, and the boy's shoulders hunched defensively; the woman chuckled:

'It's all roight boy, Oi ain't goin' ter bite yeh! Oi'm Missus Kain, 'this 'ere's moy daughter Rosie. We're goin' ter the Port, down the North – are yeh off the boats?' Curiosity gleamed in the golden eyes now:

'Boats?'

'Yeh ain't a boatee kid then?' The tousled head shook slowly. 'So where are yeh from?'

'London.'

'Lunnon? Yeh're a long way from 'ome, boy! What're yeh doin' 'ere?'

'Came up wi' me Dad, didn' I?'

'So where's 'e then?'

''E's – not 'round now.' The brown eyes regarded the boy thoughtfully:

'Not 'round? So what about you then? 'Ow're you managin'?' The shoulders under the old dufflecoat shrugged:

'I'll manage. I c'n look arter meself.' The boatwoman shook her head:

'Oi ain't so sure yeh can, lad. Not oop 'ere. Rough place, this can be. Where's yer Mam?'

'Dead.'

'Oh – Oi'm sorry, boy.' She looked around as the other boy's voice called from the stern of the boat:

'Coom on Mam! We're losin' toime!'

'You 'old on, Luke!' she called back: 'We'll be away soon

enough! You, lad:' she turned back to the boy under the bridge: 'Yeh'd as well coom with oos, eh? Yeh look frozen – 'n Oi'll wager yeh 'aven't 'ad a good meal fer a day or two, neither. Coom on, oop yeh get!' The boy shook his head, and she put her hands on her hips in that 'don't give me any trouble' pose:

'Coom on, shift yehself! Yeh can warm oop in the cabin, get some 'ot soup down yeh, 'n we'll let yeh down a bit along if yeh h'insist, roight?' The boy just looked up at her for a moment; but then the thought of warmth and hot soup won out. He scrambled to his feet, unsteady from lack of sleep; she took him by the elbow and walked him along to the stern of the boat.

'Luke! Give oos a 'and will yeh?' The stocky youth in the back of the boat leaned out and helped their passenger over the side into a little well-deck; the woman stepped nimbly over after him, and ushered him down inside the tiny cabin, where a small coal stove gave off a radiant warmth. The boat boy called out to his sister:

'Go on then, Rosie! Let's get a move on!'

The girl clucked the horse into motion again; the C-lop C-lop of its hooves rang out, echoing under the railway bridge as the towrope slowly drew tight again; a gentle surge, and the boat began to move, gliding silently beneath the girders, and out again into the brightening spring morning.

Chapter Two

'Slip that coat off, lad, yeh'll warm oop quicker without it.'

Down in the boat cabin, the woman stirred a big pot that stood on the stove, speaking over her shoulder to the brown boy who huddled on the bench behind her. Resentment stirred in him at being told what to do by a stranger, but he quelled it, recognising the sense of what she said; he wriggled in the confined space to get the dufflecoat off of his shoulders and then rolled it up, putting it on the seat at his side. Already the warmth of the cabin was seeping into him, forcing the chill of the past night deeper inside him where it made him give a last involuntary shiver.

A mug of hot steaming soup was thrust into his hands, the woman smiling down at him:

'Get that down yeh, laddie!' He took a sip, and the hot savoury liquid snuffed out the last of the bitter cold from his stomach; he took a longer swig and closed his eyes in pleasure. He heard the woman chuckle:

''Ere, lad, eat a slice o' bread with it, that'll keep yeh goin' fer a whoile.' He took the proffered doorstep-sized slice of brown bread and bit into it, suddenly aware of the gnawing hunger in him. He ate the rest, interspersing his bites with mouthfuls of soup; by the time he had finished, he was feeling warmer and more comfortable than he had been for some days. He leant his head back against the wooden wall behind him, eyes closed again.

The boatwoman had been watching him eat; now she chuckled

softly again and turned back to the stove. Ladling out two more mugs of the soup, she took them in one hand and climbed back out of the cabin into the well at the stern of the boat:

'There yeh are, Luke.' She handed one to her son and turned to look ahead: 'Rosie! Coom 'n get your'n!'

The little girl quickly ran back to the boat and grabbed the mug from her mother with a smile; she took a sip and ran forward again, returning to her place behind the horse which had kept plodding on regardless. Her mother called after her:

'Keep an eye out fer Alice at Fact'ry, roight?'

'Yes, Mam!' her voice floated back through the mist.

'You too, Luke – roight?'

'Yes, 'course, Mam!' The boy's tone was world-weary; she just smiled at him and stepped down into the cabin again, letting him take his place, stood in the stern doors, where he leant casually on the heavy wooden tiller.

''Ow're you feelin', young fella?' The boy in the cabin opened his eyes and looked up at her:

'Better.' He hesitated: 'Thanks – fer the soup, 'n that.'

'Yeh're welcome, lad. Oi'll not see a young'un loike you go 'ungry, not if Oi can 'elp it.'

'Yeah – thanks.' Another pause: 'Yeh'd better drop me orf, I'll be gettin' back.' The woman gazed at him thoughtfully:

'Back? Back to what, lad?' The boy just shrugged.

'If yer Mam's dead, 'n yer Dad ain't around no more, who's goin' ter take care o' yeh?'

'Told yeh, I c'n tek care o' meself!'

'Oh yeah? 'N 'ow old are yeh, then? Twelve, thirteen? 'Ow're yeh goin' ter manage, all alone, in a strange town, wi' no fam'ly 'n no friends, eh? Tell me that, boy!'

'I...' He stared up at her, anger in his dark eyes; but then his head fell forward and he gazed at the floor, shaking his head: 'I'll get by. Got a bit o' money in me pocket, I 'ave.'

'Oh? 'Ow mooch?'

'Never you mind! It's mine, right?' The anger was mixed with suspicion now as he looked up. The woman's eyebrows lifted:

''Course it is, boy! But 'ow long's it goin' ter last yeh, eh?'

'Long enough!' She regarded him steadily, and then went back to her question:

'If yeh've got no-one 'ere, where're yeh goin' ter go?' He just stared again, as she went on: 'If yeh've got no reason ter stick 'round, yeh could coom wi' oos. 'Ave a bit of a 'oliday, loike.'

'What? Why would yeh do that, fer me?' She laughed:

'Oh, we'll get yeh workin'! Yeh can 'elp wi' the locks, 'n walkin' wi' the 'orse, 'n in return we'll feed yeh 'n keep yeh warm. What do yeh say?'

'I dunno... Are yeh sayin' yeh need my 'elp?' She smiled at him:

'Oh, we do h'okay, me 'n Luke 'n the girls – but another pair of 'ands wouldn't go amiss.'

'So – if I 'elp, yeh'll get me dinner 'n that?'

'Fair's fair, lad.' He looked around the tiny cabin:

'Where'd I sleep, then?'

'Yeh'll ave ter share wi' Luke, in the fore-cabin. Me 'n the girls sleep in 'ere.'

'Won' 'e mind?' She chuckled again:

''E'll do as 'e's told! 'E moight be captain 's far 's the comp'ny's concerned, boot Oi'm still the boss 'round 'ere!'

'I dunno...' He gazed up into her smiling face, feeling unsure of himself. Part of him felt the urge to exert his independence, to go his own way, to become the man he aspired to be; and yet, another part of him yearned to let himself relax into the welcome he saw in her eyes, to accept, however briefly, the opportunity to be a boy again, to be fed and looked after, with nothing to worry about: 'I dunno...'

'Coom with oos, eh? See a bit more o' the country – mebbe yeh'll foind somewhere yeh'd rather be, summat yeh'd rather do, along the way.' Seeing his hesitation, she reached out to stroke his brown cheek. The boy flinched away, and she let her hand rest momentarily on his shoulder instead. At her touch, the child in him won out – but he needed to hide behind an assumed bravado:

'Yeah – okay. If yeh need my 'elp, I'll come along.' Her smile grew wider as she nodded:

'That's settled, then.' She took a quick glance out of the porthole in the side of the cabin, and turned back to him: 'Cold noight, las' noight.'

'Yeah, it was.'

'Did yeh get any sleep, there oonder that bridge?'

'Some – not much' he admitted.

'Ah.' The woman stepped past him into the forward part of the cabin, under the parted arch of lace-edged curtains, and let down a flap until it rested against her ample tummy. She groped inside, and came out with a rolled-up hessian mattress:

'Get oop a minute...' The boy stood up, and she laid it down on the bench: 'There yeh are. Kick yer boots off 'n lie down there fer a whoile.' He did as she directed, swinging his legs up beside him; he lay curled up, because the bench wasn't long enough for him to stretch out.

'That's our Alice's bed yeh've got there, but Oi don't reckon as she'll moind. You troy 'n get some sleep – Oi'll wek yeh when there's somethin' ter do.'

Chapter Three

Drowsy after the food, in the warmth of the cabin, the brown boy was asleep in minutes. The boatwoman stood watching him for a while, before tapping her son on the leg to tell him she wanted to get out of the cabin. He stood back out of the doors, and she climbed out to join him, sitting on the gunwale beside the welldeck as he resumed his place, one arm draped over the long curved tiller.

'So 'oo 'is 'e then? Did yer foind out?' She smiled at him:

'No – 'e's asleep now, mekin' oop fer lost toime. Oi'll get 'im oop ter 'elp wi' 'Ampton locks.'

''E's a boatee, then?'

'No – but 'e's said as 'e'll 'elp. You can teach 'im, eh?'

''Old on, Mam – 'ow far are we tekin' 'im?'

''E's coomin' with oos, ter the Port 'n back.' Luke just looked at his mother, a kind of resigned tolerance in his eyes. 'Well, 'e ain't got no-one. 'Is Mam's dead, 'n 'is Pa's – well, 'e says as 'e's not around any more. What that means Oi don't know – but 'e's all alone, in a strange town, no-one ter care fer 'im.'

'So yeh're goin' ter tek 'im in, are yeh?'

'No! It's joost – ter give 'im a break, toime ter think about things, mebbe decoide what 'e wants ter do.' Luke was silent for a moment, but then he burst out:

'But Mam! We don't need 'im, we don't need 'is 'elp! We're foine as we are, even without Pa, we don't need no-one else!'

'Oi told yeh, it's joost the one trip, oop ter Stanlow 'n back.'

'If 'e's off the bank, 'e should be in one o' them kid's 'omes, not gettin' in our way!' Another thought struck Luke: 'Oi suppose 'e'll be sharin' wi' me?'

'S'roight.'

'Oh, *Mam!* Yeh moight 'ave asked me!'

'There's plenty o' room, yeh've got the fore-cabin ter yerself. 'E can go on the soide-bed.'

'Oh, Mam...'

Silence fell, the boy staring ahead so as to avoid his mother's eyes, easing the heavy tiller to guide the long boat around the gentle bends of the canal, watching his little sister walking at the horse's rump away in front of them.

Around another bend, and they passed the junction where the two main lines of the Birmingham Canals met. Just beyond, under Factory Bridge, a young girl stood waiting for them, a canvas shopping bag in her hands. Rosie greeted her eagerly as she passed, slowing the horse down so that Luke could steer the boat in close to the bank. The girl stepped onto the boat's flat deck in front of the cabin, and then up onto the cabin roof. She came to the stern end and handed the bag down to her mother:

'Oi got everythin' Mam.'

'Good girl, Alice. D'yeh want some soup?'

'Yeah, please!' Luke stood back out of the cabin doors again, allowing his mother to duck down inside. Alice went to speak again as she jumped down and followed, but her mother raised a finger to her lips for silence.

'Mam's picked oop a stray' Luke told her as he saw the puzzled look on her face. She raised her eyebrows, but stepped down inside. Moments later she rejoined him, a mug of soup and a slice of bread in her hands:

''Oo is 'e, Luke?'

'We don't roightly know, Al.'

''E's *black!*' The boy laughed:

'Well, brown, anyway!'

'Oi wonder where 'e's from?'

'Dunno. Rosie found 'im – 'e was sleepin' rough under the big railway bridge, oother soide o' Tipton Turn. Mam got 'im on the boat, give 'im some soup 'n set 'im ter catch oop on 'is sleep.'

'Yeah – on *moy* bed!'

'What's she doin' now?'

'Startin' on cookin' dinner fer later.' Curiosity lit the girl's blue eyes: 'Oi bet 'e's from *Africa,* or somewhere! That's where black people live, ain't it?'

'Oi dunno, Al! Yeh'll 'ave toime ter foind out, though, Mam's tekin' 'im ter the Port with oos.'

'Really? Ooh! 'Ow old is 'e?'

'Dunno. 'bout your age, Oi'd guess.'

'Ooh...' Alice lapsed into a fascinated silence, and Luke found his annoyance with his mother's decision being overtaken by his own curiosity about their strange passenger.

Down inside the cabin, the brown boy slept on. After several nights with little sleep, the gentle motion of the boat and the whisper of water along the hull only served to deepen his slumbers; the soft bump and rocking as Alice joined them didn't disturb him, and he was only vaguely aware somewhere in his subconscious mind when she and her mother entered the cabin. And the quiet sounds and movement around him as the boatwoman sat at a stool beside the lowered flap of the table to slice vegetables and a rough piece of mutton, all of which went into a stewpot on the stove, sent him into a pleasant dream of times gone by, times in a now-forgotten home when his own mother would fuss around him...

He stirred in his sleep as a sudden darkness enclosed the boat, and the woman smiled down as he resettled himself without waking. Light dawned again as they emerged from the tunnel, and still he slept on.

Another hour passed, and a gentle hand shook his shoulder: 'Nnnh...' He rolled over.

'Wek oop, lad. Yeh've 'ad a good sleep, now's the toime yeh can mek yerself useful!' He gazed up at the figure of the boatwoman, blinking still-drowsy eyes, as she went on: 'Oi'll leave yeh to wek oop proper-loike. We'll be foive minutes ter the top 'un – there's a coop o' tea there for yeh.'

He managed a mumbled 'thank you', and pushed himself into a sitting position, swinging his feet from the bench to the floor as she clambered out into the sunlight. Feeling better rested than he had for days, the boy cupped the mug in his hands and took a draft of the tea. It wasn't like anything he'd tasted before, almost as heady as his Dad's whisky and ginger, that time he'd stolen a surreptitious sip and got a belt for it – strong and sweet, with an odd underlying flavour he didn't recognise. But nice, too – he smiled to himself, and drank off the rest of the mug although it was nearly hot enough to burn his mouth.

Putting the cup back down on the table, he took his time to gaze around him, taking in properly his strange surroundings: The little cabin was even tinier than he'd first thought. It was no more than six feet across, from where he sat, and much of that space was taken up by a kind of built-in vertical cupboard, the front of which was folded down in front of him to form the table. Below he could see a narrow drawer, and a door into the cupboard just above the floor. To the left stood the little stove, gleamingly black, on a stout shelf a foot or so above the floor, a kettle mumbling quietly to itself on the top. The stove pipe led upwards through the ceiling, taking a couple of kinks on the way, and the wall behind it was bright with a collection of fancy plates, each with a picture painted on it and elaborately pierced edges. The cabin wall next to the stove housed two small recesses, in which he could see scraps of cloth, and a metal bowl hung from its attached handle in front of them, with another brightly-painted picture of a castle and a river on its base, and painted flowers all around its rim.

The bench he had slept on ran along the other side; to his left, the cabin wall this side of the doors housed a small cupboard at the top, above where his feet had been. Light streamed through a round porthole just beside his head, sparkling on glowing brass which seemed to be everywhere – polished rails on the stove, more, bigger rails along under the ceiling over the stove, where two threadbare but clean tea-towels hung. A strip of black leather with shining horse-brasses hung alongside the door, and an ornate brass fixture on the side of the big cupboard bore an oil-lamp.

He looked to his right – there, another part of the cabin was partly hidden by a kind of cut-away wooden wall, the aperture framed with light cotton curtains edged with lace, held back in an inverted v-shape. He leant forward to peer through, and saw that the bench on which he sat continued to the far wall; opposite, another cupboard reached up to the ceiling, with a drawer below a drop-down door, and more doors above that. A voice startled him:

'That's moy bed in there, boy! Yeh shouldn't be lookin' in there.' He turned at the boatwoman's stern tone:

'Sorry, missus. Didn' know that, did I?' She stepped down to sit on the step inside the cabin doors and smiled at him:

'Yeh ain't a boatee, are yeh? No reason yeh would know. Boot remember, lad – yeh don't look inter people's bed-'oles, it ain't done.'

'Oh – okay.'

''N listen – yeh don't step on another boat, without they ask yeh on board, roight? 'N if yeh 'as ter go across someone else's boats, yeh cross over the deck, in front o' the cabin. T'ain't done ter look inter another cabin, roight?'

'Yeah, okay!' She looked at him, aware of his annoyance at being told these boater's rules:

'Well, remember what Oi said, all roight? Yeh don't want ter get yerself in trouble.'

'No – okay.' He relented, realising that she only intended to save him from possible embarrassment.

'Coom on then. We're at the top of 'Ampton...' She bent to retrieve an iron implement from below the stove and held it out to him: 'Tek this, yeh'll need it! That's a windlass – yeh 'old the 'andle, put the square on the gear ter raise the paddles – Luke'll show yeh.'

He took the windlass, none the wiser for her explanation, and followed her out of the cabin.

Chapter Four

Outside, the mist of the dawn had given way to a pleasant spring morning. The boy looked around – the scene before him was changed, but somehow the same: Black, greasy-looking water surrounded the hull of the boat still, and the buildings all around had the same grimy appearance as those he'd seen the evening before. To his right, a bridge spanned what looked like the entrance to some kind of dock; in front, the canal forked, passing under another bridge to the left while straight on led past a little row of cottages with, before them, what he knew to be a lock. Its top gate was closed against them, and Alice, at the tiller, swung the stern of the boat in against the bank:

'Go on, then! You two boys run ahead 'n set 'em, we'll bring the boat down.' The boatwoman took the brown boy by his arm: 'What do we call yeh, lad? What's yer name?' He paused while Luke stepped over the gunwale onto the towpath and looked around at her:

'Jesse – Jesse Carter.'

'Ah – roight then, Jesse. You go on wi' Luke, 'e'll show yeh what ter do.' What the boy didn't notice was the look of disgust that his older companion had given him at the sound of his name.

The two of them hurried past where little Rosie stood beside the patiently-waiting horse, to the first lock. There, several men stood talking; one of them spoke up;

''Mornin' Luke. 'Ow are yeh?'

23

'Foine, Mister Blake! 'Ow's yer locks terday?' The man laughed:

'They're all foine – but yeh've got a bad road!' Luke shrugged; then he turned to Jesse:

'This is a lock, roight?' He spoke as if to an infant, and Jesse immediately bridled at his tone:

'Know what it is, don' I? Seen 'em before, in Islington, 'aven' I?'

'Oh – yeh know 'ow ter work 'em then, do yeh?' Now, Jesse had to drop his angry gaze:

'No, I guess not.'

'Roight then, look 'ere:' Luke brandished his windlass in the other's face: 'Yeh put this square 'ole over the end o' the spindle, see?' He demonstrated, on the nearest paddle post: 'Mek sure the catch is on:' He flipped the catch of the ratchet over so that it rested on the notched shaft: 'And yeh woind the paddle oop.' He turned the L-shaped windlass around and around; Jesse watched as a toothed rack rose up past the wooden post where the spindle was mounted, making a loud clattering noise. Water began to swirl in the empty lock, pouring in through the opening sluice; he looked up with a jerk as a bang echoed from the far end of the lock. Luke laughed:

'Frit yeh, did it? S'joost the gates bangin' to – weren't properly shut, see.' He gestured to the far side of the lock:

'Now you – go over 'n get th'other paddle oop. Yeh walks across the gate!' He said impatiently as Jesse hesitated. Stung by his tone, the brown boy stepped up onto the single top gate's balance beam and walked rather unsteadily along it until he could jump down onto the ground at the far side. He put the hole of his windlass over the squared shaft as Luke had shown him – and then realised he couldn't turn it because he'd got it on the wrong way, with the handle pointing towards the post instead of away from it. The older boy's audible chuckle made him flush with embarrassment as he took it off and reversed it – now, he could wind the gear up.

But it was much heavier, much harder to do than he'd expected. He braced himself and tried again, this time starting it moving, all the time aware of the amusement radiating from the other side of the lock:

'T'ain't as easy as yeh thought, eh?' At last, Jesse got the paddle all the way open, the gear coming to the end of the long rack and stopping abruptly. He relaxed, heaving a sigh, and heard that impatient chuckle from across the lock:

'Can't rest yet! There's another twenty o' these ter go!' Luke sat with his buttocks against the balance beam where it projected beyond the lock on his side, his legs braced – in barely a couple of minutes, the water level within matched that outside the lock, and the gate swung slowly open as he walked backwards, pushing it. He stood upright again, beckoning Jesse to follow him:

'Coom on then! Mam 'n the girls'll do the rest, we've got ter get the next'un ready.' Jesse looked down at the uninviting water – with the gate now standing open, how was he supposed to cross back over?

'Yeh can get back 'cross at the other end!' Luke had spotted his puzzlement, and his tone was again hectoring. Jesse stormed down to the other end of the lock and stomped across the paired bottom gates, hurrying to follow Luke as he strode out down the towpath towards the second lock.

There, they repeated the procedure in a stony silence. Luke whipped up the first paddle, then stepped back for Jesse to cross over the gate. This time he got the windlass on correctly first time, and then put everything he had into winding the gear up as fast as he could – but he was still much slower than his companion. And this time he was ready – as the gate swung open under the impetus of Luke's weight, he set off to the bottom of the lock and crossed back over to the towpath in time to meet the older boy.

As they came to the third lock, Luke swore under his breath:

'Bottom gates is open. Moost be someone goin' down in front of oos.' He hurried down and pushed one gate most of the way shut, jumped up onto the balance beam and stepped over the gap, far above the water, to the other, pushed it too nearly shut and then came back to open the top paddle. The look on his face was almost one of approval when he saw that Jesse had already got over the lock and was ready to raise his paddle – but all he said was:

'Go on, then, get it oop!'

The far gates banged fully shut as the water poured into the lock, and soon Luke had this top gate swinging open too. While he was waiting, Jesse looked back, to see the horse and its diminutive attendant standing beside the last lock. As he watched, the little girl wound up one of the bottom paddles, and Alice came to raise the other – foam swirled in the pound between them as the lock emptied itself again, and the boat's brightly painted bow slid down to vanish from sight behind the gate.

'Coom on, we ain't got toime fer day-dreamin'!' Luke's shout brought him back to his task, and he ran along the lockside to the bottom gates, only to hear the voice he was beginning to hate again: ''N don't roon by the edge – if yeh trip oop yeh'll be in the cut!'

Jesse crossed over the bottom gates and strode off down to the next lock; Luke hurried to catch him up. Neither spoke for the next little while – four more locks were set, until, as he pushed the top gate of lock number seven open, Luke called out:

'You go on ter the next one, yeh knows what ter do by now! Oi wants a word wi' Mam.'

Rather taken aback at this sudden show of confidence, Jesse walked quickly down to lock number eight – now was his chance to show that arrogant kid! He glanced back – Luke was waiting by the last lock for the boat to catch him up. He rammed his windlass onto the nearside paddle-gear and wound it open, and then crossed over to the offside. He had the paddle halfway up when he realised that something was wrong – the lock didn't seem to be filling... He looked around, puzzled – and then saw:

he hadn't closed the bottom gates! He quickly dropped the paddle again and dashed to the far end of the lock where he heaved on one gate – the flow of water from the still-open paddle caught it and slammed it closed with a resounding crash as he emulated Luke and stepped across the daunting gap to close the other, just as that voice bellowed at him:

'What d'yeh think yeh're doin'? Yeh'll 'ave the pound empty if yeh ain't careful!' With the agility of a monkey, Luke crossed the top gate and whipped up the paddle that Jesse had dropped in his panic, the look on his face betraying his disgust with the younger boy. He crossed back over: 'Drain one o' these pounds out 'n yeh'll 'old oos oop fer ages! Fer goodness' sake look what yeh're doin'!'

'All right, I'm *sorry!* I ain't done nothin' like this before, 'ave I?'

'Tha's h'obvious!' The two glared at each other along the length of the lock; as the gate began to swing open under his weight, Luke waved dismissively to Jesse to go on to the next.

He turned and ducked under a bridge that crossed the canal there, and strode on down, fuming: *Just who does 'e think 'e is?* He reached the next lock, and stood looking at the wooden stump with its attached ironwork, the square spindle waiting for his windlass: *Why am I doin' this?* His arms and legs were both aching, and he was regretting now that he had given in to the temptation of the boatwoman's invitation. He found himself tempted to go back to the bridge, to scramble over its parapet and run off, leaving his tormentor to cope on his own. But that would be to give in, to admit he couldn't do what the other boy seemed to find so easy, and he was stubborn enough to reject that thought: *I can do it – I'll show 'im!* And anyway, his coat was still in the boat's cabin, and he'd be needing that through the chilly spring nights.

He looked up, to see Luke appear from under the bridge; he strode down and swung the open bottom gates to, then hurried back and wound up the paddle at the top. Luke stepped past him,

27

up onto the balance beam and over the lock, where he lifted the other paddle. Now, Jesse was on the side where the gate was hinged, the balance beam projecting over the towpath – he went to the outer end of it and rested his buttocks against it as he'd seen Luke do at the previous locks. Glancing across, he caught a slight, surprised smile on the other boy's face, which quickly vanished when he saw Jesse looking.

Luke walked the length of the lock and crossed the bottom gates. He turned away and went on down to the next, leaving Jesse to open the gate; as the water levels equalised, he felt the beam move under his weight – and then the gate began to slide away from him, catching him by surprise with the ease of its movement. He walked backwards, as Luke had done before, pushing with his legs, his bottom still against the edge of the beam, until the gate stood wide, ready for the boat to enter. As he straightened up, he looked around and saw the horse plodding towards him, along the side of the last lock, drawing the boat in; the little girl at its side raised a hand and waved to him, smiling, and he waved back: *She likes me, at least!* He turned away and followed Luke, feeling a little more comfortable with the situation fate had landed him in.

As the seemingly-unending flight of locks dropped down into the valley, they descended into an even more industrial scene than the one they had left; and now, before him, massive and stately viaducts, their brickwork grimed with the smoke of the trains they carried, strode across from horizon to horizon, crossing high above the canal and making the boat's progress seem insignificant. Railway lines seemed to go in all directions, at different levels, criss-crossing each other; trains, mostly of equally-grimy goods wagons, clattered and clanked their way all around him.

The two boys worked on in silence – if still not happy with his companion's presence, at least Luke seemed to have stopped his incessant sniping, and Jesse almost began to enjoy himself. He found a strange kind of satisfaction in their teamwork, walking on from lock to lock, the first to arrive closing the bottom gates while the other raised a first paddle, whoever was towpath-side staying to open the top gate while the other went on ahead. He had long lost count when the locks began to lie a little further apart, and their surroundings became more rural.

His arms and legs had stopped aching – now, they had descended into a kind of numbness that was a long way past fatigue. At last, they came around a final bend, to a lock where a heavy brick bridge crossed just beyond the bottom gates; Luke looked at him and actually smiled:

'Noomber twenny-oone! This 'un's the last!'

Jesse couldn't help heaving a sigh of relief, but there was an evil edge to Luke's chuckle:

'Oh, we ain't done yet!'

They set this last lock, and Luke led Jesse through the bridge, where he was surprised to find that the canal came to a T-junction:

'This is cut end – that's the Staffie cut. That way' he gestured to their right, where the new canal passed under another bridge: 'goes ter 'Aywood turn 'n the Trent 'n Mersey. We goes down the Shroppie...'

'That's that way, then?' Jesse looked to their left, but Luke sneered:

'No! That way goes ter Stourport 'n the Worcester River. We goes oop there a bit 'n then turns off agen.' He pointed right. Jesse felt his anger rising again, feeling that he'd been deliberately baited into getting it wrong. Luke took him by the arm and led him over the second bridge, to the towpath on the far side of the 'Staffie cut'.

There was no lock in sight:

'Where are we goin' then?'

'Ter the turn. There's a stop-lock there, 'n we'd best 'ave that ready 'fore the boat gets there.' He strode off, and Jesse hurried to keep up. He was desperate now to sit down and rest, but his stubbornness wouldn't let him even suggest the idea; and Luke didn't seem inclined to pause even for a moment.

They walked for what seemed like ages; the canal led almost straight on, under a massive railway bridge, then a succession of smaller bridges. A long open stretch, and then the towpath itself began to rise up as the channel beside them widened out. The path divided, and they turned off, passing under a stone bridge which spanned another new canal, turning to the left from the one they had been following. And another lock stood before them.

Jesse stared – this one seemed completely pointless to him. The difference in the water levels each side couldn't be more than a few inches! As luck would have it, it stood ready for them, the gate wide and inviting, and Jesse gave a silent prayer of thanks as he went and sat down on the balance beam, stretching his stiff back. Luke went back under the bridge, looking the way they had come, waiting for the sight of the horse and the approaching boat.

Chapter Five

Jesse was almost dozing in his fatigue when Luke returned. He snapped his head up as the older boy said:

'Boat's coomin. 'Bout foive minutes.' He just nodded, feeling too tired to speak. But after a brief, vaguely awkward silence, he plucked up the courage to ask:

'What's the point o' this?' He gestured at the shallow lock, half expecting another sneer from Luke, but the reply held no malice:

'S'what they calls a stop lock. It's 'cause these two canals belong ter diff'rent coomp'nies, 'n the one don't want the t'oother pinchin' their water.'

Silence fell again, and despite himself Jesse found his head nodding.

'Wore yeh out already, 'ave Oi?' He looked up; the hectoring tone was back in Luke's voice: 'Don' worry, it's a long way ter the next 'un. 'Bout two hours.' There was a challenge now in the boat boy's eyes: 'Can't 'spect too mooch from a kid wi' a girl's name, Oi s'pose.'

'What do you mean?' Jesse was stung to anger by his comment.

'Jessie. S'a girl's name, ain't it?'

'Bleedin' well ain't! J-E-S-S-E, right? Like Jesse James!'

''Oo on earth is she?'

'IT'S A HE! Jesse James was a famous outlaw, right, in America!'

'Never 'eard of 'er.'

'OH FER CRYIN' OUT LOUD! HIM, RIGHT, HIM!'

'There's no need ter shout.' There was a satisfied smirk on Luke's face now. After a moment, in which Jesse sat seething, he went on: 'Yeh still sounds loike a girl ter me.'

Jesse's temper snapped; he jumped to his feet and lashed out with a fist. Luke ducked and stood up himself; as Jesse threw another punch, he leant back away from it and caught his fist in one hand. Grabbing his wrist in the other, he twisted Jesse's arm until he had no choice but to drop to his knees. Jesse tried to head-butt him in the stomach, but Luke twisted his arm further down...

'WHAT'S GOIN' ON 'ERE?' The boatwoman's stern voice interrupted their struggle; the horse had appeared under the bridge and, as it drew the boat around the corner and into the lock, Mrs Kain left its heels and hurried towards the two boys, her face like thunder.

'Nothin' Mam. Joost foolin'.' Luke assured her. She stared at him, then turned to Jesse:

'Is that roight?' He hesitated, but then decided that it wasn't worth making an issue of it:

'Tha's right. We was only foolin' abaht.'

'Roight then.' Her stern gaze switched between them: 'Let's 'ave a bit less foolin' 'n a bit more workin', shall we?'

The boat came to a halt in the lock as Alice, who had been steering, slowed it with a heavy rope at the stern around a bollard; Prince stood patiently waiting as Luke went to close the gate behind it. Jesse picked up the windlass from the ground where he had dropped it and went to open the paddles by the other gate – in moments the water was level and he pushed one side open while the boatwoman opened the other:

'Luke? You can walk wi' Prince fer a whoile. Alice? You steer agen – Oi wants ter talk ter Jesse 'ere.' The girl stepped into the boat's stern well and took the heavy wooden tiller under one arm, but her brother groaned his protest:

'Oh, Mam!' She gave him a grim smile:

'Not too toired fer a little walk are yeh?' Jesse restrained an urge to grin as she unconsciously picked up the initial cause of their fight; the temptation became even greater as Luke retorted:

'No, 'course not!' But there was a stormy look in the glance he gave Jesse.

'You coom 'n sit down wi' me, lad.' Mrs Kain had climbed onto the flat deck of the boat; now she beckoned Jesse to join her. He clambered up onto the high deck, and sat with his back against the front of the cabin, beside the ample figure in her flowing skirt and pinafore, the strange, fancy bonnet on her head: 'So what's yer story, Jesse? 'Ow did yer coom ter be sleepin' oonder that bridge?'

'Didn' 'ave nowhere else ter go.' The boy gazed at his feet, stretched out in front of him.

'Yeh've got no-one 'round Birnigum or Wolver'ampton, then?'

'Nah.'

'So where's yer Pa?'

'Dad? 'E's... gorn away.'

''N joost left 'is son? What kind of Dad is 'e, eh?'

''E's all right!' Jesse sprang to his father's defence: ''E didn' 'ave no choice, right?'

'If you say so, boy. 'N yer Mam? She's dead, did yer say?' The boy nodded:

'Yeah. She died when I were about six – she was goin' ter 'ave another baby, but... She died.'

''N the babby?' The boatwoman's voice was gentle.

'It died too.' He bowed his head.

'Oh, Jesse, Oi'm sorry, boy.' He looked up startled as he felt her slip an arm around his shoulders, and then gave her a tentative smile:

'Long time ago, now.' He felt a rare urge to think about his mother, to remember her; his voice went on, reminiscently: 'She came from Jamaica, that's why I'm this colour, I'm 'alf black.

Dad, 'e was a sailor, merchant navy, 'n 'e met 'er there when 'is ship docked. Went back there again, 'n married 'er. Brought 'er back ter England with 'im.'

''N then yeh lost 'er?' He nodded again:

'Yeah.' He looked up into the boatwoman's sympathetic smile, realising the reason for his sudden rush of nostalgia: 'You remind me of 'er. She was a... big lady, too.' She laughed:

'Don' be shy about it, lad, Oi knows Oi'm a big girl!' She regarded her companion for a moment: 'So yeh've really got no-one? No aunties or ooncles?' He shook his head.

'So what were yeh goin' ter do?' she asked; he shook his head again:

'Get me some kind o' job, somewhere. I'll get by, 'til Dad comes ter get me.'

''N when's that loikely ter be? Days, weeks, moonths?' She could barely hear his reply:

'Dunno. Long time, prob'ly.'

She held him close in sympathetic silence for a while, as the boat glided along through open farmland, the rippling of water along the hull only adding to the tranquillity. Seventy feet in front, the stocky pony kept up an easy, steady pace, encouraged along by the sound of Luke's footsteps at its heels.

Before long Jesse looked up, the feelings of hopelessness that had gripped him briefly now past. He leant back into the boatwoman's ample shoulder, and took in his new surroundings properly for the first time. In front of his stretched-out legs, the boat seemed to go on forever; long and very narrow, it tapered into the distance. Several flat wooden hatches sat on the deck, which he now saw had a gentle curve from side to side, and at the front, another small cabin stood about a foot higher than the deck – Rosie sat on one side of it, and now she caught his eye and waved. He waved back, looking at the various things which stood on the deck – about in the middle was a big wooden barrel, and in front of it an odd structure with tapered wooden ends and a canvas cover, rather like a small tent. In front of that, a mast stood up with the towrope attached at the top, leading off to the back of the horse's ornate harness.

He looked over his shoulder, getting a shy smile from Alice as his eyes met hers. Behind him, the bigger cabin was a bit higher than the forward one, and its roof followed the inward curve of the hull below it. Alice stood in the small well behind it, the long curved tiller under her arm leading back to a massive wooden rudder. Everything was brightly painted, and spotlessly clean. He turned back to Mrs Kain, and she chuckled at the enquiring look in his eye:

'Yeh'll be woonderin' about oos, will yeh?'

'Yeah – 'oo are yeh, where're yeh takin' me?' The doubt and anxiety was back in his voice.

'Yeh're safe with oos, boy.' He tone was gentle: 'Oi told yeh before – Oi'm Missus Kain, 'n them's moy kids. Luke, 'n Rosie, 'n...' she gestured over her shoulder 'Alice. We works fer Clayton's, roight? Thomas Clayton's, from Ol'bry, 'though it's Mr Forrester as roons things now. Ol'bry's back near ter Birnigum, roight? We does a reg'lar trip, down ter the Port – Ellesmere Port, roight? That's boy the Ship Canal, 'n we 'as ter go be'ind a tug out on it ter the h'oil wharf at Stanlow. They loads oos wi' fuel oil, 'n then its back be'ind the tug ter the Port, oop the locks there 'n back 'ere. We h'unloads at Langley – that's oop a stretch we calls The Crow, at Ol'bry – then down agen ter Clayton's dock 'fore we goes off agen.'

''Ow long does all that take?'

'Oh, 'bout a week. Depends on when we catches the tug, mostly.' He sat quiet trying to take this in whilst having no idea about the places she'd named or where they might be. Another question occurred to him as he thought about her family:

'What about yer 'usband, Missus Kain? Where's 'e?' She sighed softly:

''E's dead, loike yer Mam, Jesse. 'E got killed in the winter.

That's whoy Luke 'as ter be captain, official-loike, 'cause Clayton's won't 'ave a woman as captain. 'E's too young, really, 'e's only fifteen, boot we told 'em 'e were sixteen, 'n they agreed that were old enough ter be captain. Yeh see, we'd 'ave lost the job, 'n the boat, ootherwoise. 'N that's our 'ome, too.'

'You 'aven't got a 'ouse?'

'What use would that be ter oos? We're on the move all the toime! No boy, we lives 'ere in the boat. Me 'n the girls in this cabin, Luke in the littl'un oop the fore-end. And yeh'd best coom 'n 'ave a look at where yeh'll be sleepin' fer a noight or two!' She stood up and turned to help Jesse to his feet: 'Coom along wi' me.'

Chapter Six

Jesse followed the boatwoman along the deck, carefully stepping around the various obstructions on their way. Rosie stood up as they approached, smiling rather nervously at the strange boy:

'Go 'n tek a look at the stew, Rosie.' She went, reluctantly, to do as her mother told her. Mrs Kain slid back a hatch in the roof of the small forward cabin and led the way inside, down a few steps. When Jesse climbed down after her, he found himself in what looked like an even smaller version of the other cabin. About the same width, but a lot shorter, this one also had a bench to one side, faced by a little pot-bellied stove, and across the rear half a flap was lowered to form a bed across the boat, with a horse-hair mattress laid on it:

'That boy!' His mother tutted: 'Can't be bothered to put 'is bed oop! Yeh'll 'ave ter manage on the soide-bed' she indicated the bench: 'It's a bit short for yeh, but if yeh sleep curled oop, yeh'll do.'

'Yeah... It'll be better'n sleeping under bridges. Thank yeh, Missus Kain.' She reached into a drawer under the bench and pulled out another mattress, sensing the lack of enthusiasm in his voice:

'There's a mattress for yeh. Is soomat wrong, lad?'

'No! No, that'll be fine, thanks.'

'Coom on boy – what's oop?'

'Well – this is where Luke sleeps?'

'Yes, that's roight.'

'Well – I don' think 'e likes me very much.' She regarded him for a moment:

''E doesn't think Oi should 'ave brought yeh along. Since 'is Pa doied, 'e's got ter thinkin' of 'imself as the man o' the fam'ly. You learn 'ow we works the boat 'n do your bit, that'll be the way ter get 'im on your side.'

'I've been doing that! But I made some mistakes, I suppose.'

'Y'ain't been on a boat before, 'ave yeh? Well, yeh've got a lot ter learn! You joost do yer best. Oi'll tell 'im ter go easy on yeh.'

They climbed out into the daylight again, and walked back along the deck. Mrs Kain disappeared into the cabin again, saying that she was going to put some potatoes in the oven; Jesse sat down again, his back against its front wall. He watched the steady plodding of the horse, away in the distance in front of the boat, the stocky figure of Luke striding out just behind it, and relaxed, enjoying the spring sunshine. The day was getting warm now; he stripped off his woollen pullover and dropped it by his feet. He was almost daydreaming, and looked up in surprise as someone sat beside him.

''Ello.' The girl's voice sounded shy; he smiled at her:

''Ello.' He saw her flush slightly and look away. She watched the countryside drifting past them for a minute or so, then turned back to him:

'That's a lovely shirt.' He nodded, looking down at the bright check of navy blue, red and white:

'It's one my Dad got me, not long before 'e went away.'

'Oh. Oi'm Alice.' He smiled again, and this time she smiled back.

'I know. I'm Jesse – Jesse Carter.' She looked at him, chewing her lower lip nervously, then spoke cautiously:

'Jesse – that's a foonny name fer a boy, ain't it?' There was none of the malice of Luke's comments in her tone, and he found it easy to take no offence at her question:

'Not really. My Mum chose it, she came from Jamaica.'

'Oh.' There was a pause before she asked: 'Where's Jamaica? Is it in Africa?' He laughed:

'No! It's an island, near America.'

'Oh.' Another pause: 'Do black people live there too, then?'

'Yes – it's mostly black people there, I think.'

'You didn' coom from there then?'

'No. I was born 'ere, in London. My Dad was a sailor, see? He married Mum and brought 'er back here. She died when I was six.'

'Oh – sorry.' He shrugged:

'Long time ago.'

''Ow old are yeh now?'

'Thirteen. 'Ow 'bout you?'

'Oi'm twelve. Luke's fifteen, 'n Rosie's noine. 'Ave you got any brothers or sisters?'

'Nah.'

'Where's yer Pa? Is 'e dead too?'

'Nah. 'E's 'ad ter go away fer a while.'

'What's 'e do?'

''E's – a driver. Drives cars fer people.'

'Oh.'

The pause this time felt easy, friendly. At last Alice spoke again:

'Moy Pa were killed. Back in the winter.'

'I'm sorry, Alice. Yeh miss 'im?

'Yeah. We're h'okay, now the coomp'ny's set Luke on as captain, we can roon the boat, the four of oos. Boot Oi do miss 'im.'

'What 'appened to 'im?'

''E was on the h'ice-breakin' boat. We was froze oop at Ol'bry, 'n they was troyin' ter break through. 'E slipped, fell off 'n got caught 'tween the boat 'n the h'ice. They took 'im ter 'orpsital, but it weren't no good.'

Jesse caught the slight slump of her shoulders, and slipped his arm around them to comfort the girl. She looked up with a surprised smile, then dropped her eyes again. They sat together in silence as the boat travelled on; Jesse threw a glance back over his shoulder, unsure of what the boatwoman would think of him with his arm around her daughter, but the look in her eye was one of amusement as she stood at the tiller, Rosie sat on the gunwale at her side.

In front of them, the canal stretched on and on in a nearly straight line. Framed in the bridge which was approaching them rapidly, he could see that it sank into a long cutting. They passed under the bridge, and the air became noticeably cooler as the sunshine gave way to shade; Alice gave a slight shiver, and Jesse tightened his arm about her shoulders, receiving another shy smile from the girl. Neither of them noticed Luke glance back, checking the progress of the boat, or caught the anger in his expression when he saw his sister with the boy's arm around her.

They travelled on. Jesse had felt their progress to be unbearably slow – he was used to travelling by car, or on the train – but as he got used to their pace, he began to realise that in fact the landscape was floating by them with a steady inevitability, that they were making mile after mile more quickly than he'd thought. The cutting went on for more than one of those miles; they passed by a town, peering down at them from above, and then at last the cutting gave way to open country again. Now they were travelling along the top of a high embankment, with astonishing views of the flat countryside around them. They passed under a couple more bridges; and then, to Jesse's surprise, the canal led over a bridge – looking down, he saw a long straight road going underneath them. An Albion lorry was approaching, and he waved back as an arm came out of the window at the sight of the boat, feeling amazed that they could actually go over a road while sitting on a boat.

Soon after, the canal was back in another cutting; a couple more bridges cast their shadows on them, and just beyond the second, he saw another lock appear in front of them. His windlass still lay on the cabin roof where he'd put it down; he took his arm from around Alice's shoulders and stood up, picking it up as he did so. Mrs Kain steered the boat in close to the bank, and he jumped off at her nod to hurry forward and help Luke set the lock.

Neither of them spoke as the lock filled; Luke heaved the top gate open and Prince, at his call of 'Go on then!', walked forward and drew the boat in. Luke closed the gate again, and waved Jesse to go to the far end of the lock. He watched, and copied his companion's actions as he wound up the bottom paddle. In moments, the boat was sinking rapidly into the brick-lined cavern of the lock; Luke went to lean against the end of the balance beam at his side, and Jesse again copied him. He felt the gate slowly easing as the weight of water came off of it; and then it was swinging open, almost of its own volition. Alice had stepped off the boat before it sank below the lockside; now, she took over Luke's place at the horse's heels, clicking her tongue to get him moving. Rosie was nowhere to be seen; Luke jumped down onto the boat's deck:

'Coom on, 'less yeh wants ter get left be'ind!'

Jesse jumped down after him, jarring his heels as he landed heavily and getting a scornful look from the older boy.

'Yeh can tek it easy fer a bit now – 'bout foive hours ter Tyrley 'n the next'uns' Mrs Kain told him from the tiller: 'Dinner'll be ready soon. We eats on the move, h'okay?'

'Yeah, that's fine.' Jesse suddenly realised how hungry he was.

'Luke, you coom 'n steer.' The boat boy stepped up and walked over the cabin roof, jumping easily down into the stern well and taking over from his mother who disappeared inside. Jesse sat down again where he had before, and watched a little village slip past, a garage and wharf beside its bridge. Then the boat was slowing again, and Luke steered in close to the edge; now Jesse spotted the little girl on the towpath, weighed down by an enormous can, as brightly painted as anything else on the boat. She heaved it up onto the cabin roof, and then stepped back on board herself; Luke moved the can across and placed it in front of the stove's chimney, to his left. Rosie climbed up onto the roof and came and sat on its edge, next to where Jesse sat on the deck below her:

''Ello – Oi'm Rosie.' She betrayed none of her sister's nervousness with him; he grinned up at her:

'I'm Jesse.' She nodded:

'So Oi 'eard. It's a...'

'Funny name fer a boy, I know! Like I told Alice, me Mum came from a place called Jamaica, 'n she chose it. It's American, really.'

'Ooh! Are you American, then?'

'No, I'm English, like you. My Dad was English, see?'

'Oh – yeah.'

'That can you were carrying, it did look 'eavy – what did yeh 'ave in it?' She gave him a surprised look:

'That's ar water-can. What we keeps ar fresh water in. Fer drinkin', 'n washin-oop 'n things.'

'Oh – right.' It hadn't occurred to Jesse to wonder where they would get water from, on the boat – now he realised that although they were surrounded by the stuff, the water from the canal would hardly be fit to drink: 'Where do yeh get it from?'

'There's taps, 'ere 'n there along the cut. Oone's there, by the lock at Wheaton Aston. We fills the can oop whenever we can, yeh see.'

'Oh – yeah, I see.' Another thought occurred to him: 'Where do yeh go – you know?' She stared at him for a moment, puzzled; and then the light dawned:

'Ter the toilet, yeh mean?' She chuckled: 'There's a boocket, in the fore-cabin. Oonder the soide-bed.'

'Oh – hey, that's where I'm sleepin'!' She chuckled again:

'It's all roight, it's got a lid on it! 'N we don't use it any more'n we 'ave to, ter save 'avin' ter h'empty it all the toime. You boys are lucky, yeh can 'ave a pee any toime yeh want.'

Jesse felt rather relieved as Mrs Kain interrupted their conversation, appearing from the cabin with two big plates. She put one down on the hatch lid in front of Luke and handed him a fork, and then beckoned Rosie:

'This'n's Jesse's. Oi'll 'ave yours in a minute, loove.' The little girl carried the plate to him, with another fork stuck into the piled-up stew, and then went back for her own.

Jesse started eating, and found the stew to be delicious – meat and carrot and parsnip and other vegetables, with a thick, tasty liquor, and a big potato in its jacket. He looked up with a satisfied smile as Rosie came and sat down again, her own plate in her hands.

Chapter Seven

They ate in silence, Jesse relishing every mouthful, aware that he hadn't been eating so well for the last few days. Mrs Kain had taken over the steering from Luke while he ate, sitting on the gunwale at one side of the stern well. The Staffordshire countryside continued to pass them by, under the bright spring sunshine; when they'd cleaned their plates, Mrs Kain collected them again as Luke returned to his steering:

'Rosie, you go 'n send Alice back for her'n.' The little girl got up and turned to Jesse:

'D'yeh want ter coom wi' me?'

'What?'

'Coom wi' me 'n walk wi' the 'orse fer a whoile.'

'I dunno...'

'Oh, coom on! If yeh gets toired, yeh joost waits fer a bridge-'ole 'n gets back on the boat.'

'Yeah, okay then.'

He stood up; Luke steered in to the bank, and he followed Rosie as she jumped off. The two of them ran forward to catch up with Alice and the horse; Rosie called back over her shoulder to him to be careful and not trip up. The canal here was running through another deep cutting; they caught up with Alice, who ruffled her little sister's hair in greeting and gave Jesse another shy hello; he responded with a breathless smile.

A little way in front of them, a bridge spanned the cutting, the channel narrowing beneath it. When they reached it, Alice stopped, waiting by the edge, and as the boat ran past her she jumped onto the deck. Jesse had been watching over his shoulder; he heard Rosie chuckle:

'See? Yeh can get back on anytoime there's a bridge-'ole, Luke'll coom in close for yeh when 'e sees yeh.'

'Yeah, right.'

They walked on in a friendly silence for a while. The towpath was very variable – in places it was wide and smooth, but all too often the water's edge was broken away, leaving a narrow and uneven path where the horse picked his way carefully, and they had to walk in single file. They came to a wide stretch, and the little girl fell into step beside him:

'It's noice 'avin' you with oos. We only sees oother folks at the stops, usually.'

'It was nice of yer Mam ter invite me along. Even if Luke doesn' like it!'

'Oh, 'e'll be all roight.' They walked on for a bit before she said:

''E ain't been the same since Pa got killed. 'E used ter be mooch more fun.'

'I s'pose 'e thinks 'e's got ter be grown up now. Yer Mam said 'e's the captain now?'

'Ah, yeah!' Rosie's tone was derisory: 'Mam's still the boss! S'only 'cause she can't be captain, 'cause she's a woman, roight?'

'Yeah, she tol' me.'

''E used ter mek me laugh, foolin' 'round; 'n 'e'd grab me 'n tickle me. 'E 'asn't doon that fer ages.' She looked up at him: 'Mebbe you can cheer 'im oop a bit?' Jesse laughed:

'I told yeh, 'e doesn't like me much!'

'Oh, 'e'll coom 'round, give 'im toime. Oi think yeh're noice!' He laughed again:

'Thank you, Rosie! But I'm only stoppin' with yeh fer a bit. One trip, ter wherever it is yeh're goin' 'n back, that's what yer Mam said.'

'Oh – yeah.' She fell into a disappointed silence beside him.

On and on they walked; the cutting gave way to another high embankment where they could see for miles over the surrounding fields. The canal cut straight across the landscape; soon, it was carving its way through another stretch of higher ground in yet another cutting. They passed under an occasional bridge; another came up before them, and Jesse was astonished when the horse plodded up the ramp which led over it. Rosie sensed his puzzlement, and laughed:

'Joost watch!' They followed the horse over the bridge; on the far side of the canal, as the boat drew closer beneath them, Prince followed the path down the other side, now going back towards the boat. But as the ramp reached ground level again, he turned right around and strode out, passing underneath the bridge now. He drew ahead, until the towrope tightened, and then slowed his pace to the same steady plod as before.

'That's clever!' Jesse exclaimed, astonished at the way the design of the bridge itself allowed the horse to change sides of the canal without having to detach the towrope.

'Tis, ain't it?' Rosie chuckled.

So on they went. Another half-hour passed; they were passing through another long, deep cutting, when Jesse realised that the canal vanished into the hillside in front of them.

'What 'appens now?' he asked. Rosie's reply was scornful:

'S'only a little tunnel.'

As they approached the tunnel, Jesse could see the daylight at the far end – not so far away, just as Rosie had said. He peered into the blackness, feeling unaccountably nervous of it, but Prince just kept plodding on, apparently unconcerned at heading into the hole in the hillside. Rosie followed the horse into the darkness, and Jesse kept pace with her; but she'd sensed his doubts:

'Don' worry, this'n ain't 'aunted!'

'Haunted?' She chuckled at his surprise:

'There's some o' the tunnels as are. Or so they say, any'ow.'

'Are there many o' these?'

'Not this way, there's only this'n 'n 'Coseley.' Rosie sniggered: 'You was asleep when we went through that'n this mornin'!'

'Oh, right.'

'Soomtoimes we 'as ter go a diff'rent way, 'n there's a big 'un that way, at 'Arecastle. They 'as a tug there ter tek the boats through, but it's a real long walk over the top. But that's foine by me, that'n is 'aunted 'n Oi don' fancy walking through it!'

And then they emerged into the daylight again, the horse trudging on without pause. Rosie took Jesse's arm and halted him where there was a bricked edge to the towpath; the boat emerged from the tunnel and Luke swung the stern in close to the bank. Alice stepped off the boat and hurried on to follow Prince while Rosie jumped up onto the deck. Jesse, feeling weary again after walking a fair few miles, quickly scrambled up to join her. They sat side by side on the cabin-top, their feet on the boat's deck; Luke, relieved from steering for a while by his mother, passed them without a word and went to the fore-cabin where he let himself part-way down the hatch steps and stood there, shoulders protruding into the daylight, watching the world go by.

The little girl gave her companion a quick smile:

'Tell me more 'bout you' she asked. He shrugged:

'Ain't much ter tell.'

'Yeh coom from Lunnon?'

'Yeah. We lived in Islington, tha's in the north part of London. Dad rented a 'ouse there, 'n I went ter school a few streets away.'

'Yeh went ter school?' Her intrigued tone puzzled Jesse:

'Yeah, 'course! All kids 'ave ter... oh!' It suddenly occurred to him that the child at his side clearly wasn't in school: ''Ow do you...'

'We don'. Oh, we gets a day or two, now 'n then, when we're toied oop – can't when we're goin', can we? Yeh can read 'n wroite, then?'

'Yeah, 'course!' Jesse's flash of indignation faded into a kind of guilt as he realised that the little girl beside him obviously couldn't. After a thoughtful silence, she asked:

'What's it loike, goin' ter school ev'ry day?' He shrugged:

'Okay, sometimes. I liked some of the lessons – geography's good, learnin' about other places. 'N science. Woodwork 'n metalwork, too, I'm good at that sort o' thing. But...'

'What didn' yeh loike?'

'Well – I didn' get on wi' the other kids...' He hesitated before explaining: 'They didn' like me, I s'pose. 'Cos I'm black. They use'ter pick on me, make fun o' me, even get together 'n beat me up, sometimes.' Rosie was staring:

'Joost 'cos yeh're black?'

'Yeah.'

'Well Oi never!' She looked at him, her head tilted to one side: 'Oi don' care what colour yeh are, Oi loike yeh.' He turned to her with a smile:

'Yeh mean that?'

''Course! Yeh're noice!' She paused and then asked: 'Whoy'd yeh coom ter Birnigum?'

'Things went wrong, 'n Dad come 'ere ter find a noo job, like.'

'Then 'e 'ad ter go off? Was that fer 'is new job?'

'Er – yeah, kinda.'

'What 'appened ter you?'

'Um – well...' He seemed reluctant to tell her, but after a moment he went on: 'Some people let me stay wi' them, but I didn' like it there.'

'So yeh ran away?' Rosie sounded thrilled at this romantic idea; he chuckled:

'Yeah. Few days ago. I been sleepin' rough since then.'

''Til we found yeh oonder that bridge!'

The silence that fell now was friendy and companionable. Prince kept up an easy pace, drawing the boat along at a good speed, Alice striding out to keep up with him; an almost proprietory smile hovered around Mrs Kain's face as she regarded the two figures sitting in front of her, and Jesse relaxed, enjoying both the tranquillity of his surroundings and the lifting of responsibility from his shoulders, even if it was only temporary. Only the sight of Luke's hunched and hostile back spoiled his equanimity.

The hours passed; the day continued bright and warm, even if a chill remained in the air whenever the boat ran though one of the long, deep cuttings which were such a part of the canal. But at other times, they were floating along the top of high embankments, basking in the sunshine. For the first part of their journey since leaving Wolverhampton they had seemed to be alone on the waterway, but now they began to meet other boats. Some were horse-drawn, like their own, but others had engines whose heavy exhaust beats disturbed the quiet of the countryside and echoed along the cuttings; these mostly were towing a second unpowered boat behind them. And almost all of the boats Jesse saw were riding low in the water, clearly heavily loaded, unlike their own. Every boatman, leaning on his tiller, raised an arm in greeting with a cheerful ''ow d'yer do?', and Mrs Kain would call back – Jesse soon took to waving back, following Rosie's example.

Eventually, they emerged from another spectacular cutting, carved out from solid rock, around a long bend in the canal, to see, through the arch of a bridge, another lock before them. Everyone except Jesse had clearly anticipated this – Luke had already emerged from his perch in the fore-cabin, his windlass stuck in the back of his belt, and as they approached the bridge he went to jump down onto the towpath. Jesse too stood up, and picked up the windlass he'd left again on the cabin-top; Mrs Kain gave him an approving look:

'Good lad! Go on wi' Luke. There's foive 'ere, 'n that's it fer today, we stops ternoight in Drayton.' He nodded, and jumped off under the bridge to follow Luke as he hurried forward to the lock.

They quickly worked the boat through the five locks; evening was drawing in as they cleared the last, and Jesse realised that the day was almost gone. And barely half an hour later, with the darkness now all but complete, they stopped between a succession of bridges, in what looked like a bustling town, opposite a busy boatyard. The boat was soon securely tied, and, at their mother's urging, the two girls led the horse away.

'We puts 'im in the stables at noight, where it's warm, 'n 'e can rest 'n eat' Mrs Kain explained to Jesse: 'Bread 'n cheese fer supper? There'll be a 'ot pot o' tea, too.'

'Thanks – that sounds great!'

'Roight – you go wi' Luke 'n sort yer beds out, Oi'll give yeh a shout when it's ready.'

Chapter Eight

Rather reluctantly, Jesse walked to the front of the boat, where Luke had already vanished into the small cabin. He was about to climb down the steps when he recalled Mrs Kain's words about etiquette on the boats; he hesitated, then knocked on the hatch-cover. Luke's head appeared; a look of surprise crossed his face when he saw Jesse standing there.

'Can I come in? Yer Mam said ter sort me bed aht.'

'Yeah – roight.' Luke stepped back down, and Jesse followed him inside. In the tight confines of the cabin, Luke had his own bed set out – as his mother had observed earlier, he'd never folded up the drop-down door which usually concealed it during the day, but now he had straightened the mattress and laid a tired but clean blanket out on top of it. Jesse's mattress lay on the side-bed where Mrs Kain had left it; Luke opened the door into the cupboard above his own bed and reached inside:

''Ere yeh go. Blanket for yeh – still gets chilly of a noight, but we'll be cosy enough in 'ere wi' two of oos.'

'Thanks, Luke.' Jesse was consciously on his best behaviour in an attempt to achieve some degree of truce at least with the other boy: 'Look – it was yer Mam 'oo asked me ter come with yeh. Weren't my idea.' Luke turned to look at him:

'Yeah, Oi knows that. But listen 'ere – *we don' need yeh,* roight? Whatever Mam moight 'ave told yeh, we roons this boat joost foine on ar own, see?'

51

'Yeah, I know, I can see that. But – I'm 'ere now, fer a while any'ow, 'n I want ter 'elp where I can.' Luke held his gaze for a moment:

'Yeah. H'okay, but...' He was interrupted by a knocking on the cabinside, and looked around in annoyance. He climbed the steps and looked out;

'Yeah? What can Oi do fer yeh?' Jesse could hear a man's voice respond from the bank:

'This is the barge *Murray*, is it?'

'S'what it says there.' Luke's tone was belligerent.

'All right boy, I just want to ask you something!'

'Go on then?' He climbed out to stand on the fore-deck, and Jesse went to follow him, curious to see what was happening.

'We're looking for a young boy, a runaway, and there's a report that he might be with you on this boat.'

Luke's hand was on Jesse's head, preventing him from emerging from the cabin:

'Oh? 'Oo told yeh that, then?'

'The lock-keeper in Wolverhampton saw him with you, this morning.' The man's voice was impatient.

'Oh. Black kid, roight?' Jesse's heart sank – *he's going to give me up to them!* But Luke went on: ''E was with oos, if it was 'im. But we left 'im there, roight? 'E joost give oos a 'and down the locks, me Mam slipped 'im 'alf a crown fer 'is trouble.'

'You left him in Wolverhampton?'

'Oi joost told yeh! At Cut End, bottom o' the locks. Whoy are yeh so keen ter foind 'im, then?'

'He's run off from his foster home – and he stole some money from them, too.'

'Oh, roight. Well, 'e ain't 'ere, any'ow.'

'All right, young man. Thank you, anyway. Good night.'

''Night, constable.'

Footsteps faded away down the towpath, and Luke climbed back down into the cabin. He regarded Jesse with new interest:

'Yeh 'eard all that, did yeh?' Jesse just nodded. 'Roon away, did yeh? 'N pinched soom money inter the bargain, eh?'

'They was treatin' me like shit! 'N I didn't take much, just enough ter keep me goin' fer a while, 'til I could find a job or somethin'.'

'Ah.'

'Luke – why did yeh tell 'im that, 'bout leavin' me back there? Yeh could've 'anded me in.' The older boy laughed:

'We don' loike the 'thorities on the bank mooch! We don' go out of ar way ter 'elp any of 'em, don' matter if it's police or the canal coomp'ny's men, or the 'ealth inspectors.' This last had Jesse guessing:

'Elf inspectors?' An image of little men with pointed ears and notebooks sprang to his mind.

'Yeah. From the pooblic 'ealth h'office. They cooms ter check the boats, mek sure they're fit ter live in. Goes out o' their way ter cause trouble, most of 'em.'

'Oh, I see.' While he was absorbing this information, a call came from the stern of the boat:

'Luke! Jesse! Supper!'

'Coom on, Oi'm 'ungry!' Luke almost ran up the steps this time; Jesse followed, looking around quickly to make sure the policeman had gone, and hurried after him to the other cabin. Alice and Rosie were already there, back from settling Prince in the stables, sitting side by side on the side-bed; Mrs Kain handed each boy a plate with two thick slices of crusty bread and a slab of cheese:

'You two sit out there, h'okay?'

'Yes, Mam.' The curved wooden tiller was upturned now, pointing toward the sky to leave the well behind the cabin clear for them; they sat, one each side, on the gunwale edge: 'Did yeh see the copper, Mam?'

'What copper was that, Luke? What did 'e want?'

'Oh, nothin' mooch. Joost walkin' by, Oi reckon.'

'Ah. Interferin' beggars.' Her tone was indifferent: 'Tuck in, both of yeh – then get ter bed. We starts early in the mornin's, yeh see' she told Jesse.

'Sure thing, Missus Kain.'

''Ow are yeh h'enjoyin' it?' He smiled at her:

'It's – different! I've seen barges before – there's a canal near where we used ter live, in Islington, 'n I've seen 'em goin' through the locks there. Never thought I'd get ter go on one o' them!' She pursed her lips, but Luke's voice cut her off before she could say anything:

'Listen – this ain't a barge, roight? Barge's is big things, what they use on rivers 'n round docks 'n things – their men go 'ome at noight, they ain't proper boaters! This is a *narrerboat,* okay?'

'Oh – yeah, right, sorry!' Mrs Kain stepped in to restore the peace:

'Yeh weren't ter know, lad. Most folks on the bank gets it wrong.'

'I'm sorry – I'll remember now!' A thought occurred to Jesse: 'I've seen – narrowboats – before; but they always had a kind of open space, with cargo in and canvas covering it?'

'That's roight, boy. These'ns are different – Clayton's carry liquid cargoes, yeh see. Loike Oi told yeh before, we gets loaded wi' h'oil at Stanlow, they poomps it in from the 'finery, then it gets poomped out agen when we gets back ter Ol'bry. Oonder there' she pointed to the long deck in front of the cabin: 'it's loike big tanks, roight?'

'Yeah, I see! 'Ow much oil do yeh get in in one go?'

''Bout twenty-foive ton.' She chuckled: 'Yeh'll see the diff'rence, then! Yeh won' 'ave ter cloimb oop ter get on the boat! We 'aven't passed any oother Clayton boats terday, 'ave we?'

'No, Mam' Luke confirmed; she went on:

'Yeh'll see one or two termorrer, Oi 'spect, Jesse. You look 'ow deep they are in the water – that's 'ow we'll be on the roon back.' She sat back, a satisfied look on her face: 'H'important work, this is. 'N if there is another war coomin' it'll be all the more h'important then!'

'D'yeh think there will be?'

''Oo knows, lad. Politicians'll work that out, ain't mooch ord'nary folks loike oos can do 'bout it.'

'Yeah, I s'pose so. If it does come, I 'ope I'll be old enough ter go – I wants ter be a pilot, fly fighter 'planes. 'Ave yeh seen that noo one they got? Spitfire – Dad showed me a picture o' one. Amazin'!' The boatwoman gave him a sober look:

'Oi wouldn' be in sooch a 'urry ter go ter war if Oi were you, lad...' She hesitated, but then went on: 'Yeh moight not be coomin' back. Look what 'appened last toime!'

Chapter Nine

*Jesse peered blearily around through the tears in his eyes.
Everywhere, all he could see were officials and uniforms,
and the harsh looks of the people sitting in the huge darkly-
panelled room:*

*'Dad! Dad!' Only his father smiled across at him – but
even his smile was weak and sad.*

A hand was on his shoulder:

'Come along Jesse – come with us.'

*'No, I won't! Dad!' But his father was gone from his sight.
The hand was shaking him now:*

'Coom on, wek oop will yeh!' He opened one eye:

'Nnnh...'

'Coom on! Toime we was movin', Mam'll be after oos else.'
He opened the other eye and peered around, puzzled to find himself
in a tiny wooden-walled room, curled up on an equally-tiny bench
with a rough blanket thrown over him. The laugh that met his
ears was rough but sympathetic:

'Wek oop will yeh! Yeh're on the *Moorray,* wi' me 'n Mam
'n the girls, 'n it's toime ter get goin'!' Memory came flooding
back – waking under the bridge with the huge horse towering
over him, the big buxom boat-woman, gliding along the canal in
the spring sunshine with the little girl by his side, and Alice's shy
smile whenever she looked at him. And working the locks with
Luke, the older boy's disdain and irritation...

He swung his feet to the floor, reaching for his pullover:
'Yeah, okay! I'm 'ere now.'

After supper, they'd sat talking for a little while, and then he and
Luke had gone off to the fore-cabin to go to bed. Both had slept
in their shirts and trousers, only kicking off their boots and slipping
out of their outer clothes – but it had been warm in the tiny cabin,
and Jesse had slept only fitfully, troubled by his dreams.

Luke quickly pulled on his boots, threw on his coat and departed
up the steps into the fresh morning air, cramming an old flat cap
on his head. Moments later, Jesse followed, stepping out into the
cold light of the dawn, the sun not yet in evidence. He walked
quickly to the stern of the boat, where Mrs Kain stood in the
hatches with a steaming mug of tea. She handed another to him:

''Mornin' Jesse – 'ow'd yeh sleep?'

'All right, thanks.' He took a grateful sip. He ventured a smile
at Luke, perched on the gunwale at the far side of the little well-
deck, but the other boy didn't respond. Mrs Kain asked:

'Ready fer anoother day?' He smiled at her:

'Yeah – I guess so!'

'Good lad! We'll be ter Chester ternoight, with a bit o' loock.
'Ow'd yeh loike ter go wi' the girls 'n gear the 'orse? See 'ow
it's doon?' He grinned now:

'Yeah – that'd be good.' The boatwoman bent down to the
open doors:

'Alice! Rosie! Go 'n get Prince out o' the stables, 'n tek Jesse
wi' yeh ter see what ter do.'

'Yes, Mam.' Alice emerged, flashing a shy glance and a gentle
smile at the boy: ''Mornin' Jesse.' He smiled back:

'Good mornin' Alice. 'Ello Rosie!' The little girl followed her
sister out of the cabin and gave him a cheeky grin – both were
already in their working clothes, warm coats around them in the
chill air.

He quickly finished his tea, and turned to follow them along the towpath and up over the bridge to the boatyard and stables on the far side of the canal. Rosie grinned up at him:

'What do yeh think o' Prince?' The little girl didn't wait for an answer but chattered on gaily: ''E's lovely, ain't 'e? Best 'orse we've 'ad, Oi reckon. Pa said as 'e's a... What was it?' Alice smiled indulgently at her little sister:

'A Dales Pony, 'e said that's what the man told 'im.' She lifted her smile to Jesse, but looked away as he smiled back. Rosie prattled on:

'Yeah, that's roight! A Dales Pony. Pa said as 'e's joost roight fer ar job, 'cos 'e's strong but not too big, see? 'E can fit oonder the bridges, even on the Birnigum cut, but 'e can pull the boat, even wi' a full load, and really crack on! You saw 'im, yesterday!'

'I did...' Jesse agreed, catching Alice's amused expression and grinning back at her. Rosie wasn't done yet:

''E's mooch better'n Mabel, ar last 'orse. She was h'okay, but not as good as 'im! She took a look oop near the Port, 'n caught the newmoany. Pa 'ad ter 'ave 'er put down, 'n then we got Prince.'

They'd reached the stable yard; Alice lifted the bar across the doors, and Jesse pulled one side open. They stepped into the warm stable, smelling the aromas of straw, hay and horse. The girls led him over to the stall where the stocky black pony stood waiting patiently for them; he gave a soft whinny as Alice went up to him and stroked his muzzle. Rosie slipped an old blanket off of his back and folded it up before reaching up to fetch parts of his harness from the hooks along the wall.

Jesse hung back – out in the open, he'd been quite happy to be near the horse, even if the closest he'd been was a few feet behind, walking with Rosie. But here, in the close confines of the stall, he found the sheer bulk of the big pony quite daunting. Alice turned to him and beckoned him over – not wanting to appear afraid in front of her, he took a step closer, and she took his hand, put it on Prince's muzzle. The horse made a quiet chuffing sound, and Alice smiled:

''E loikes you!'

''E does?' Plucking up his courage, Jesse stroked the coarse hair up his nose, and Prince flicked his ears with pleasure. Alice picked up his halter:

'We'd better get on or Mam'll be mad.' She led the horse out into the open area of the stable, and Rosie followed, weighed down with the jumble of harness. Jesse stood and watched as the two girls quickly fitted each part: The heavy collar over his shoulders; the straps across his back and the trailing lines along his sides, bright with the coloured bobbins which protected his flanks from getting rubbed; the spreader which joined them behind his rump and the leather straps which kept it in place. In bare minutes, he was ready for his day's work, and Alice led him out into the brightening morning.

Rosie closed the doors behind them, and ran to catch up as they headed back over the bridge:

'Mam's got soom crochered ear-caps fer 'im, but we only put them on in the summer, ter keep the flies out of 'is ears' she declaimed breathlessly.

''E looks real smart any'ow' Jesse said, winning a delighted grin from the little girl, and another shy smile from her big sister.

Back beside the boat, Luke was waiting, looking annoyed:

'Coom on, 'urry oop! We're late!' His mother gave him a stern look from the tiller but didn't say anything as Rosie quickly took the towline from the fore-deck and hooked it to the spreader of the harness. Alice clicked her lips, and the big pony set off, leaning into the collar to take the strain until the boat began to move, slowly at first but with gathering momentum. The girl walked along behind as he got into his habitual steady stride, and Jesse went with her:

'Do yeh mind if I walks with yeh fer a bit?' She glanced across:

'No – Oi don' moind.' He looked over his shoulder; Mrs Kain was steering the boat, with Rosie in the well beside her, and Luke was sitting on the deck in front of the cabin, studiously looking away from them.

Neither spoke for a while, but Jesse caught an occasional quick flash of Alice's eyes in his direction. He wanted to talk to her, but found himself stuck for conversation. His usual interests, cars and aeroplanes and football, would have had no relevance for the girl at his side – her world was so far removed from his own, and he racked his brain for a way to bridge the gap. At last, his curiosity about that world took over, and at the same time solved his problem:

'Are there any more locks up this way?' She gave him a quick smile:

'Oi thought yeh'd ask that! Yes, lots of 'em.'

'Oh..' She actually chuckled now:

'Don' worry, they ain't as bad as 'Ampton! There's foive at Adderley, them's next, 'bout an hour from 'ere. Then it's 'alf an hour ter Audlem – there's fifteen there, but they're easy ter work. Then a bit less than an hour ter 'Ack Green Two. S'easy then, all the way ter the riser at Bunbury.'

Jesse paused – none of the place names meant anything to him, but that he'd expected. Some of the other terms, though:

'Riser? What's that? Is it a lock that goes up instead o' down?' Alice gave him a smile which had an element of her sister's usual cheeky grin in it:

'No! Yeh don' know, do yeh? It's a double lock, what they calls a staircase – two locks, but without a space in between, roight? One goes straight inter the oother.'

'Oh – right...' Jesse tried to imagine what she described, but found it hard to envisage – but he'd see for himself later in the day. Alice went on:

'All the locks are down'ill, 'til we gets ter the river. Then they're all up'ill on the way back. On the river, we gets towed by the tug, along ter the 'finery at Stanlow where they fills us oop wi' h'oil. Then we teks it back ter Birnigum, oop the Crow ter Langley.' She was echoing what her mother had told him the day before, but he nodded:

'Yeah, I see. Then yeh goes back fer another lot?'

'S'roight.'

Another odd phrase Rosie'd used came back to him:

'Your old 'orse – Rosie said she'd "took a look" – what does that mean?' Alice giggled:

'It's what we say when someone falls in! Takin' a look in the cut, see? Poor old Mabel – she caught a chill, 'n it turned inter Newmoany. We 'ad ter stay at Chester fer two days, but she didn't get better. Dad called the company 'n they got oos Prince. Mabel 'ad ter be put down. She was a good old 'orse – we'd 'ad 'er fer ages, since Oi was little.'

'I'm sorry, Alice.' She looked at him with a sad little smile:

'Rosie's roight, moind. Prince is a better 'orse – 'e's so strong! 'N 'e's real friendly, too. Mabel'd give yeh a nip if she was in a bad mood, but 'e never does that.'

They walked on in silence for a while – but it felt easier, more friendly, now, and the occasional look Alice threw in Jesse's direction was warmer, less nervous.

Chapter Ten

The town was far behind them now, the canal again running through open country in splendid isolation. The weather was rather less idyllic, though – low cloud drifted overhead, occasionally thickening into a grey blanket which threatened but did not actually drop any rain on them. Trains rattled their way along the railway which ran parallel, until the canal sank into a shallow cutting again and their noise was lost. Almost an hour after they'd left Market Drayton, the sides of the cutting gradually levelled out, and then, through a bridge, they could see a lock before them.

'Better get me windlass!' Jesse threw a grin at his companion; Alice smiled back:

'Go on then!' She kept the horse walking on towards the lock as he ran back to the boat, keeping away from the water's edge, mindful of the warnings he'd received. Luke hurried towards him, and brushed past:

'Coom on, 'urry oop!'

'I'm comin'! Got ter get me windlass, ain't I?' He grabbed it from Rosie's hand as she held it out for him, standing on the fore-deck of the boat:

'Thanks, Rosie!' Then he was rushing back, overtaking Alice and the horse, to the lock where Luke already had both paddles up. The older boy gave him an angry look:

'Yeh should 'ave yer win'lass wi' yeh – wastes toime 'avin' ter go back fer it.'

Jesse felt his own anger soar, but he kept it in check:

'Yeah – sorry, I didn' think.'

'Yeh're s'posed ter think! Yeh're the one as 'as been ter school, ain't yeh?'

'Yeah, but...'

'Yeh 'as ter think when yeh're boatin' – think a'ead 'n be ready fer the next thing, roight?'

'All right! I didn' know these locks were 'ere 'til Alice tol' me, did I?'

The lock was full now, and Luke, pushing the gate open, just glared at him. Jesse stormed off, crossed over at the bottom gates, and strode down to the next. He had one paddle up; Luke pushed past him to cross the gate and raise the other.

They went on in a strained silence, setting each lock and leaving it ready for the boat to slide in; behind them, Mrs Kain and the two girls worked the boat through, keeping pace with them. As it descended in the fifth and last lock, Jesse stood by one bottom gate waiting for the boatwoman's instructions, but Luke went to jump down onto the deck.

'Luke! You go wi' Prince now, give yer sister a rest!' He stopped, standing on the edge of lockside, but Jesse called down to her:

'Let me, Mrs Kain? I'm enjoyin' the walkin'.' She looked at him doubtfully, and he went on, remembering what Alice had told him: 'Luke can tek over arter the next ones, all right?'

'If yeh're sure, boy?'

'Sure – please?'

'H'okay then.'

'Can Oi walk with 'im, Mam?' Rosie perked up.

'H'okay. Alice, you coom 'n 'elp me get the dinner on.'

'Yes Mam.' She gave Jesse a smile as she jumped down onto the boat's deck and walked back to join her mother in the cabin. Luke jumped down too, and refitted the heavy tiller ready to steer the boat out of the lock; Jesse and Rosie pushed the gates open and hurried down to where Prince was waiting:

'Go on then! Walk on!' Rosie called out to him, and the big pony leant into his harness, stepped on, leant again, and began to walk ahead as the boat gathered way at the end of its long towline. Jesse still held the windlass in his hand, and Rosie grinned at him:

'Stick it in yer belt, that's what Luke does. It's what Pa used ter do, too.' He wasn't sure quite what she meant, and she giggled: 'Coom 'ere!' He stopped, and she went behind him, took the windlass from him: '''Old yer coat oop out o' the way!' He did as she told him, and she pushed its central angle down inside the waistband of his trousers at the small of his back. He dropped his coat over it again, feeling it settle into place, surprised at how comfortable it felt there:

'Yeah – that ain't too bad!' Rosie giggled again:

'Keeps it 'andy fer when yeh needs it, Pa said.' She walked ahead, catching up with the horse, and Jesse hurried after her. He chuckled:

'Need it agen soon, won' I?' She looked at him, surprised, and he explained: 'Alice tol' me – there's some more locks soon, ain't there?'

'Yeah, s'roight. Audlem – fifteen o' them.'

'''N this time I'll be ready for 'em! That'll stop Luke 'avin' a go at me.' The little girl looked at him:

'''E ain't all that bad really, yeh know? 'E joost...'

'Don' like me!'

'No, t'ain't that! 'E feels loike 'e 'as ter be in charge, now Dad's not 'ere. 'N...'

'''E don' like 'avin someone around who don' know what ter do. I don' belong 'ere, do I?'

'Don' say that!' She rounded on him: 'Oi loike it, 'avin you with oos! 'N Alice loikes yeh, too.'

'Yeh reckon?' She giggled again:

'Yeah! She ain't usually so shy – Oi reckon it's 'cos she *loikes* yeh!'

'Oh! Oh...' He fell silent for a while, before admitting: 'Well,

I guess I likes 'er, too. But don' you go tellin' 'er, right?' Rosie just smiled cheekily at him. 'Promise me, Rosie?'

'Maybe...' Her smile was wicked now.

'Please? It'll only cause more trouble wi' Luke!' She giggled once more at this:

'Oi think it's a bit late ter be woorryin' 'bout that. He was watchin' yeh, walkin' with 'er terday. 'N 'e saw yeh yesterday, wi' yer arm around 'er!'

'That was 'cos she was upset, 'bout yer Dad!'

'Oi'll believe yeh.'

'Oh 'Ell!' Jesse didn't need anything else causing friction between him and Luke, but it seemed he'd inadvertently done just that. He fell silent, wondering what he could do to ease the tension.

They were on a long straight stretch of canal; coming towards them was another boat, a motor boat, the sound of its engine reaching them through the cold air. As it drew close, they could see the butty following behind – both were deep-loaded, and Jesse realised they were tank-boats, like the one he was on, their holds decked over in the same way. Then they were passing, keeping over to allow the horse-boat to hold to the towpath side. A hand was raised from the tall, grey-haired man at the tiller, and he called over:

''Ow do! Yeh've a bad road, Abel's in front o' yeh!'

'Roight y'are!' Rosie called back. They exchanged waves with the young boy at the butty's tiller, and heard the distant voices as Mrs Kain and the boatman conversed in passing. They travelled on for about a quarter of an hour more, and then they rounded a gentle bend in the canal, to see the next lock in front of them, a bridge just below it.

Jesse left Rosie with the horse and strode out ahead of her. He was winding up the first paddle as Luke caught up with him and dashed across the gate to raise the other. As the lock filled, the older boy looked over at him.

'Was that better?' Jesse asked.

'Yeah.' The response was grudging, but then Luke went on, in a more conciliatory tone: 'Yeh can' afford ter waste toime, boatin'. We don' get paid 'til we h'unloads, see, so the longer we takes about gettin' there the worse it is.' Jesse was amazed at this:

'You 'as ter go all the way, there 'n back, wi' no money?'

'S'roight. Tha's 'ow it is, 'ow it's always been on the cut. We gets paid so mooch a ton, fer the trip, but only when we gets emptied.'

'I didn' know that...' Now Jesse understood a little better the other boy's annoyance at any delay, however small. But Luke wasn't making it easy for him:

'Lot you don' know, ain't there?' Jesse kept a hold on the anger that threatened to escape, staring moodily across the lock; but then he nodded:

'Yes there is! But I'm trying to learn, if you'll let me!' It was Luke's turn to gaze at him, holding his tongue for a moment. At last he too nodded, and a half-smile crossed his face:

'Y'are, Oi'll give yeh that. Mam says Oi should go easy on yeh, 'cos yeh ain't a boatee.'

Jesse felt the gate give under him, and walked backwards, pushing it open, as Luke hurried down the far side of the lock, crossed over the bottom gates and walked on to the next, visible through the bridge. He whipped up the paddle; Jesse joined him, crossed to the far side and raised that one; and so they worked on without a word, alternating each side of the locks as they came to them. But their silence was a bit easier this time; Jesse no longer felt that the older boy was watching him so closely, ready with a critical comment – and he managed all of the fifteen without making any mistakes.

Between locks twelve and thirteen, they passed under a bridge with a pub close by, then by an old wharf with a tall red-brick warehouse beside it, a massive church towering over the little community. And then they were at the last of the locks. They stood by each side, watching the boat approach and slide easily into the chamber. Each time he saw it, Jesse felt a sense of wonder that Mrs Kain, or anyone for that matter, could steer such a long vessel so neatly between the two walls, with just inches to spare, that it didn't even touch either side. And the way she casually dropped the heavy rope over the little stump on the end of the gate, so that it slowed and then stopped the boat at the same time as slamming the gate to behind it... He thought again of Luke's retort – there really was so much he didn't know about this boating business! He could drive a car – his father had taught him, not long before – but he would never dare to try and steer this boat, especially not into a lock!

Then the boat was sinking down before him. Prince stood ready, patient as ever, waiting to haul it out and set off along the next level stretch of canal – what had Alice said? All the way to Bunbury, wherever that was. Luke strode down, ready to follow the horse; Rosie had jumped onto the boat; then he and Alice pushed the bottom gates open and jumped down themselves.

Chapter Eleven

Once again, they had left civilisation behind them and were gliding along through wide pastoral landscapes, where cattle grazed the open fields on both sides of them. The day was becoming greyer as time went by, and now a gentle drizzle began to fall, not heavily but with that penetrating dampness that seems to chill the bones. Rosie had ducked down inside the cabin with her mother, and their soft chatter drifted up through the open doors; Alice stood at the helm, leaning in the hatches, a bonnet just like Mrs Kain's crammed on her head, her coat pulled tight around her shoulders; Jesse sat beside her on the gunwale, his own coat drawn up around his neck.

'Yeh can go insoide wi' Mam, in the dry' the girl suggested, but he shook his head:

'Nah – I'm okay. I likes the fresh air.'

''Ave yeh got a 'at?' He shook his head again; she called down inside the boat:

'Mam! Is Dad's old 'at anywhere? Jesse's gettin' wet oop 'ere.'

''Old on love!' came the reply, and a few moments later a hand appeared, holding an old trilby hat that had seen better days. Alice grabbed it:

'Thanks Mam!' She handed it to Jesse: 'There yeh are, that'll keep the rain off.' He took it hesitantly:

'This was yer Dad's?' She nodded. 'Are yeh sure it's okay fer me ter wear it?'

''Course! Mam wouldn'a let yeh 'ave it else.'

'Oh – right.' He put it on gratefully, although his hair was already pretty damp – it was a bit on the large side, but comfortable enough. He smiled at the girl: 'Thank yeh.' She gave him her usual shy smile in return.

They floated on through the drizzle for a while, Jesse thinking about the girl beside him, how she must feel about the loss of her father, only brief months before. He wasn't sure if he should broach the subject, but eventually he asked:

'Yeh must miss him – yer Dad, I mean.' She turned sorrowful blue eyes on him:

'Oi do, all the toime. But – 'e's gone, 'n we 'as ter get on wi' things.' She shrugged: 'Nothin' we can do 'bout it.'

'I suppose...' Jesse looked away, feeling her sadness and sorry that he'd caused it.

'Jesse?' He looked up at her again as she spoke, to see a gentle smile on her face: ''Ow 'bout you? Yeh've lost yer Mam *and* yer Dad, ain't yeh?'

'Well – kinda, I s'pose...' He hadn't thought of it that way: 'I mean, yeah, me Mum's dead, 'n Dad – well, 'e ain't around right now, so I s'pose yeh're right, in a way.'

'Where is yer Dad? What's 'e doin'?'

''E – just 'ad ter go away, fer a while. 'E'll be back, one day, 'e promised. Then 'e'll come 'n find me, 'n we'll be tergether, fer always.'

''E's workin' yeh said?'

'Er – yeah, kinda...' Alice could see both the hurt and the reticence in his eyes, so she asked no more – but she was puzzled at what she saw as very strange behaviour for a devoted father.

They glided on in a silence that was pleasantly companionable despite the cold and the damp. Jesse gazed ahead, along the gentle curves of the canal, watching Luke striding along at the horse's hindquarter, his hands in his pockets, his cap pulled down tightly over his ears. Following a long sweeping curve to the left, they passed under a road bridge built on the skew, and then the canal became impressively straight for a mile or more in front of them. A couple more smaller bridges; and then, on a long open stretch, another horse-drawn boat was approaching them. As it drew closer, the little girl walking with its horse reached up to the bridle and brought the horse to a halt; the boat's steerer held out to the far side of the channel as it drifted on, the towline going slack and falling into the water. Luke encouraged Prince to walk faster, and Alice held the *Murray* in close to the towpath; they passed the horse, and the little girl waved; then the boat was alongside them. Jesse saw the name painted on the side of the cabin – *Fellows Morton & Clayton Ltd.*

'Two's ready for yeh!' The man at the tiller called across, a hand held up with two fingers raised. Jesse bridled at what he took to be a rude gesture, but Alice called back:

'Thank yeh, Mister Atkins!' She'd seen Jesse's expression, and giggled: 'That means 'e's left two locks ready fer oos' she told him, and he grinned at her:

'I thought 'e meant – you know!' A thought struck him: 'I didn't think there were any more locks for a bit?'

'Yeah – there's 'Ack Green Two, 'bout 'alf a moile away.'

'Oh – yeah, yeh did tell me, but I'd fergot.' She chuckled again:

'Thought yeh'd got it easy 'til Bunbury, did yeh?' He nodded ruefully, but asked:

''Ow far are they?'

''Bout two 'n a 'alf hours after these'n's. Oother soide o' Nantwich.'

Another bridge was approaching, and now he could see the lock a little way beyond it. He reached around for the windlass he'd left on the cabin roof and stuck it in his belt as Rosie had shown him, and then stood up; at the bridge, Alice swung the stern of the boat in against the bank and he stepped off. He heard her giggle again as he almost lost his balance and fell, and looked around with a rueful smile before he hurried on ahead.

Luke had left Prince to walk on alone, and was already at the lock, standing by the open gate dropping the paddle on that side; he looked up as Jesse joined him:

'Roon around 'n drop that oother paddle, will yeh?' Jesse ran the length of the lock, crossed the far gates and back along the other side; he quickly dropped the raised paddle there, and stood waiting as Prince walked the length of the lock, drawing the boat in behind him; he stopped, without instruction, just far enough beyond to allow the boat to stop before it touched the bottom gates as Alice dropped the strap around the top gate's stump and snatched it closed behind her. Luke strode along the lock, gesturing for Jesse to go with him; they raised the bottom paddles, each side, and watched as the boat sank into the chamber.

This time, with the locks set for them, there was no need for the two boys to go ahead and get the next one ready. Once the bottom gates were open, Luke waved Jesse to walk around the lock again, back to the towpath side; he did so and followed Luke, heading for the second lock. There, he did what he had done at the first and walked around, crossed over and walked back to drop the far paddle. Moments later, Prince and the boat were approaching, and he marvelled again at the casual way Alice steered it into the narrow chamber and stopped it with the heavy strap. They worked the lock as they had the last; Jesse felt a suppressed pride as he caught the look, speculative but almost approving, on the older boy's face. As the boat descended in the lock, the weight of the water gradually came off the gates as he leant with his bottom against the balance beam until it gave and he swung it quickly open before jumping down onto the deck. Luke hurried off to catch up with Prince, who was already setting off on his own, and they were away again, towards the town of Nantwich.

Less than an hour later they were passing the town on a high bank, a wooded stretch to their left as they gazed down on the houses to the east of the canal. They floated over another aqueduct, Jesse staring down in amazement once again as he watched a couple of cars travelling underneath them. Then under another bridge, painted white, more massive than those he'd seen before.

Passing the town, the canal had taken several quite sharp turns; now, it began to meander around the countryside, in distinct contrast to the long straight stretches and gentle bends he'd become used to. The channel seemed wider too. Alice was steering again, Jesse sitting at her side, enjoying their quiet companionship; the drizzle had tailed off and stopped again although the heavy cloud remained when she stepped back out of the hatches. Mrs Kain emerged, with two plates of stew:

''Ere yeh go, kids. Get stoock in!' Jesse took his gratefully and sat back on the gunwale as she ducked back down inside; Alice put hers on the slide-hatch and began to tuck in. In minutes their plates were clean; Alice looked at him with a grin:

'That's better, eh?' He grinned back:

'Sure is!'

Rosie popped up out of the cabin and retrieved their plates; moments later she was up again. Alice steered the boat to the side; she stepped off, making a more elegant job of it than Jesse had done earlier, and ran off to catch up with Luke. They walked on together until a bridge appeared around the next bend, where Luke stopped at the side until the boat caught up with him. He jumped onto the deck, came over the top of the cabin and went down inside with a hungry grin as Alice stepped out of the way. Mrs Kain emerged again, her hands full of steaming mugs:

'Tea!'

'Thanks Mam!'

'Thank yeh, Missus Kain.' The boatwoman turned to face forwards:

'Rosie! Tea!' Her voice went up a register, to carry the distance; the little girl looked around and ran back. She took her mug with a breathless 'thanks Mam' and ran back to catch up with Prince. The boatwoman put a hand on her daughter's shoulder:

'You get down insoide 'n warm oop a bit. You too, Jesse.' Alice nodded gratefully and ducked out of sight, but Jesse stayed where he was:

'I'm fine here, thanks. If yeh don' mind?'

'Yeh sure, boy?' She shrugged in response to his nod, and tucked the tiller under her arm.

'Missus Kain?'

'Yes, lad?'

'The canal looks – different, here.' She laughed:

'Yeh're an observant oone, ain't yeh? That's 'cos it is, boy! This lot's mooch older, it were built oop 'ere from Chester ter start with, 'n the rest, all the way ter Birnigum, weren't built 'til later. Locks are diff'rent from 'ere too, they're woider, teks two boats in at oonce. Yeh'll see, when we gets ter Bunb'ry!'

They were just passing another junction in the canal; Jesse could see locks climbing away from them towards the west, and he asked:

'Where's that go?'

'That's the Welsh cut – goes ter Ellesmere, 'n then crosses inter Wales, goes ter Llangollen. Used ter go ter Welshpool 'n all, but a bank give way a whoile back, 'n that way's closed now.'

She settled herself in the hatches, giving the brown boy a cheerful smile which he happily returned. Looking up at the sky, he reckoned it must be about mid-day; the cloud was thinning at last, and he could make out the sun's position, high in the southern sky. They travelled on, and again he felt a kind of amused surprise at the way the boat seemed to be eating up the miles despite their apparently slow progress. He found himself daydreaming, relaxed and comfortable as the day warmed up around him, wondering what it would be like to live this life all the time... But he was only along for the one trip. Then back to Birmingham, find some kind of work, and maybe a place to sleep other than the streets, while he waited for his Dad to come back. He hadn't admitted it, but he knew in his heart that that would not happen for a long time, years even – so he had to make his own way, somehow. That thought began to depress him again; but then a shaft of sunlight broke through the cloud, suddenly warming his back, and he pushed the thought away: *Worry about that later! Just enjoy this while you can...*

The boatwoman had seen the smile cross his face:

'Yeh h'enjoyin' yerself, Jesse?' The smile grew wider as he turned to look at her; he nodded:

'Yeah – thanks. I'm beginnin' ter envy you, doin' this all the time!' She laughed:

'T'ain't alwes loike this, lad! Yeh want ter be out 'ere in the snow 'n oice, when there's a blizzard blowin'. Gets dangerous as well as h'oonpleasant, then. Yeh knows what 'appened ter moy man?' Jesse felt a surge of sympathy for the stoic, capable woman at his side:

'Yeah – Alice tol' me.' She nodded, and smiled at him:

'Yeah. But it's a good loife, most o' the toime. We're ar own bosses, pretty well, 'n we ain't stoock in some fact'ry, day in, day out, loike lots o' folks. Settle ter this, could yeh?'

'I dunno... I want ter be a driver, like my Dad, really. I already knows lots about cars, 'n engines – I can drive a car, 'n 'e's showed me ways ter make 'em go faster.'

'Yeh loikes h'injuns, do yeh?' He nodded eagerly, and she gave him a thoughtful look: 'Ah... Yeh're a good lad, Jesse...'

They floated on, and he turned to watch the countryside drifting past, patches of sunlight occasionally relieving the gloom, until the boatwoman gestured in front of them. He looked up, to see a huge building apparently blocking the way, and stared in amazement. Mrs Kain saw his expression and laughed:

'We goes oonder there! Look, yeh can see the arch.' He looked, and sure enough there was an arch like a bridge cut out of the building where it stood over the canal: 'It's a ware'ouse, see? Boats can get emptied oonder it, roight inter the stores. But we goes right on through.'

And so they did. Beyond the warehouse, Prince paced up the slope of a big bridge, over the top and down the other side; beneath it as they passed, Jesse could see another branch canal leading off, to the east this time. Before he could ask, the boatwoman told him:

'That way goes ter Middlewich 'n the Trent 'n Mersey cut. We goes that way soometoimes, if there's a stoppage along this way – yeh can get ter Birnigum, but it teks longer.'

Chapter Twelve

The rest of the day followed much the same pattern. The youngsters shared the task of walking with Prince through the afternoon, as the skies brightened slowly; the cloud never cleared completely, but the occasional flashes of sunshine lifted everyone's spirits. Jesse found himself enjoying life on the boat more and more, the regular work of the locks interspersed with long relaxing periods of travel, gliding along in silence or walking behind the horse, usually with little Rosie at his side. Luke's mood seemed to remain one of easier tolerance, even if he still refused to show the younger boy any kind of real welcome; and Jesse tried to avoid anything which might aggravate him – he handed Mr Kain's trilby back to his widow once it seemed clear that the rain was going to leave them alone, and kept a discreet distance from Alice, letting her go on alone when it was her turn to follow the horse.

At Bunbury, he saw for himself what she'd meant by a 'riser'. The first of the bigger locks, it was an impressive structure after the narrow ones he had become used to. Twice as wide, massively built; and with a second chamber directly below the first, which necessitated working the water levels carefully, as the first drained into the second. And then on, slowly down into the Cheshire plain, some of the locks spaced well apart, but two of them within sight of each other. The second of these caught his attention – it seemed to be built of metal rather than brick or stone, and he asked Luke about it as they raised the paddles. The older boy laughed:

'Yeah! Got this'n wrong, didn' they? The ground 'ere's very soft, 'n it kep' shiftin'. Lock kep' fallin' in, 'n they kep' on rebuildin' it, 'til someone thought o' makin' it out o' h'iron instead. Still didn' work, moind – it's still 'ere, but it's moved all the same. Yeh can' barely get two boats through at once, 'cos the soides 'ave coome in. Oi've 'eard as folks 'ave got stuck 'ere fer an hour or more.' He chuckled again at the thought.

One more single lock, and then Jesse found himself walking for eight miles. Rosie started out with him, but she got tired and he sent her back to the boat to rest, and went on alone. Despite the depredations of several nights spent sleeping rough, he was still quite fit, and took the hike in his stride, enjoying stepping out at a good pace to keep up with the black pony, who seemed completely tireless.

Evening began to draw in; they passed a small village, and then ran into what appeared to be the outskirts of a town, past an old wharf that looked to be derelict. And then another lock; five, in quite quick succession, through leafy suburbs, and then they were in the industrial heart of the town. A wide stretch of canal, warehouses and factories around them, and then a high cliff towering over them on their left, a wall at its top. Darkness had fallen by the time they reached a wide basin, a lock visible beyond it; here, Mrs Kain called out to Alice to bring Prince to a halt, and they tied up for the night.

She had come up with mugs of soup during the afternoon, and now set about getting bread and cheese ready for the hungry crew's supper while the girls again took the horse off for his night in the stables. The two boys sat in the stern well as she bustled about down in the cabin:

'Luke?' Jesse wanted to express his relief that they seemed to be on better terms now, but didn't know how to put it into words.

'Yeah?' The fifteen-year-old's reply was taciturn.

'I – I'm pleased we seem to be gettin' on better terday.'

'Hnh!' Luke didn't seem to agree, but then he said: 'Yeh're learnin'. Lookin' what yeh're doin' 'n thinkin' ahead.'

'But yeh still don' like me bein' 'ere?' Luke just shrugged.

Plates with slabs of bread and chunks of cheese appeared in front of them, and then the girls were back, brightening the mood with their chatter. A mug of tea, and then they were despatched to bed; Jesse stripped down to his vest and underpants, having been too warm the previous night, and he noticed Luke doing the same, but the older boy just responded with a grunted 'g'noight' to his attemptedly friendly 'sleep well'.

He woke more easily the next morning, having slept much better, as Luke was dressing. He waited until the other boy climbed the steps and disappeared into the morning before swinging his feet out of bed and dressing himself, aware of the tight confines of the tiny cabin.

Mrs Kain had mugs of tea and slabs of bread and butter ready by the time he joined them around the stern cabin in a bright but chill dawn and wolfed them down gratefully. The girls went off to fetch the horse, but he and Luke took their windlasses and walked down to the top of the lock he'd seen the previous night. What he saw now took his breath away: Not two but three massive locks, built as another 'riser', descending into what looked like a huge hole in the ground. He stood gawping, until Luke nudged him grumpily:

'Coom on, we got work ter do!'

'Er – yeah, right...' That feeling of awe stayed with him as they filled the top lock and Luke swung one of the massive gates open; and then they were walking down, ready to empty it into the middle chamber. He called across to Luke:

'These are amazin', ain't they?' But he elicited only a shrug in response.

Half an hour later, they were setting off out of the bottom

lock. Now, Jesse could see that in fact the canal, which had appeared to stop in a blank brick wall, actually took a sharp turn to the right beneath the railway which passed overhead on a solid viaduct. Rosie was walking with the horse; Alice tucked the tiller under her arm after heaving it out to swing the stern around the tight corner; her mother, below in the cabin, began to prepare the main meal, and that left Jesse and Luke together, standing on the boat's long deck. Jesse went to sit down by the front of the cabin, but Luke strode off towards the fore-end, ignoring him. He hesitated, and then followed him, determined to try and clear the air between them as much as he could. Luke turned and sat on the top of the little fore-cabin, and frowned discouragingly as he saw Jesse approaching. Jesse ignored his expression, and sat down beside him:

'Luke – I know you don' like me bein' 'ere, but can' we try ter be a bit more friendly?' The older boy turned and stared at him for a moment; then he burst out:

'Listen – yeh're roight, Oi don' loike yeh bein' 'ere, Oi don' *want* yeh 'ere! 'N Oi ain't yer friend, roight?' Jesse went to apologise, to try to placate him, but Luke didn't give him the chance: 'We don' need yeh, we can get on foine without yeh! Don' you dare wear moy Dad's 'at again, roight? It were 'is, 'n you don' touch it! 'N you keep away from moy sister – she's only twelve, 'n she ain't fer the loikes o' you any'ow!' He paused for breath, but Jesse was too astonished to be able to reply: 'Oi'm the captain 'ere, 'n you'd better do as Oi say! Or Oi'll let the cops know where you are, 'n they'll soon 'ave you away, roight?'

This threat brought Jesse's temper to boiling point, and before he could stop himself he'd snapped back:

'You better watch yerself 'n all! If I tell your comp'ny you're only fifteen, they'll 'ave you off this boat! You won' be no captain any more then, will yeh?'

Luke stared at him again:

'You wouldn' dare! They wouldn' listen ter you, any'ow.' But he sounded uncertain, his temper dampened by Jesse's words. A tense silence ensued, until Jesse said:

'I'm only 'ere 'til we gets back ter Birmingham anyway – what's that, another few days? You keep off my back, 'n I'll keep off yours, okay?' Luke continued to stare, but at last he agreed, reluctantly:

'All roight. But you still ain't moy friend, h'okay?'

'Okay.' Jesse felt disappointed that he hadn't achieved more – but at least it sounded like a truce.

After another two hours of travelling through wide flat countryside, eventually a cluster of brick buildings appeared beyond a hump-backed bridge. They passed under its arch, to see more locks before them, but Rosie brought Prince to a halt at the top of them where a number of other boats waited. Greetings were exchanged with the other boaters, and Jesse found himself being introduced to a bewildering array of other families. Directly in front of the *Murray* were two more tanker boats, also with the *Thomas Clayton (Oldbury) Ltd* name on the cabinsides, and the short stocky captain shook Jesse's hand vigorously:

'Coom along fer the roide, 'ave yeh? These'n's are moine – we'll be goin' down the river wi' yeh termorrer!' He'd been introduced as Mr Beechey; the names on the boats were *Stour* and *Hudson,* and when Jesse asked, he was only too proud to show off his 'injun':

''Ow 'bout that, boy? A Bolinder, that is, ruddy good injuns they are. Better'n a 'orse any toime!' He said the last with a broad grin at Mrs Kain, who retorted:

'But we don' 'ave ter put oop with the smell o' gas-oil all the toime, Abel!' It was obviously a long-standing if cheerful disagreement; the boatman laughed:

'Yeh'll 'ave ter give in oone day, Annie! Yeh knows the coomp'ny wants h'all motors on this run!'

'Oi'm quoite 'appy wi' moy 'orse, thank yeh Abel! We don'

want no smelly, noisy h'injun, do we, girls?' Alice and Rosie nodded their agreement:

'No, Mam!'

Jesse, still peering into the engine-room of the *Stour,* wasn't sure he agreed – the big single-cylinder diesel was unlike any engine he'd seen before, but it was quite impressive with a lot of polished brass and copper fittings around its massive green-painted bulk. He turned to Mrs Kain:

'Are we stayin' 'ere fer terday then?'

'S'roight. Tugs don' work on Soondys, see? We'll be down ter the 'finery in the mornin'. Don' tek long ter fill oos oop wi' h'oil, 'n we'll be back ter Chester wi' any loock termorrer noight.'

He nodded – he'd lost track of the days, hadn't realised it was the weekend.

Chapter Thirteen

Halted by necessity, the various boaters took the opportunity to catch up on a range of delayed jobs. Mrs Kain, along with a number of the other women, had her dolly-tub out and began to wash her family's spare clothes; men were to be seen diving in and out of engine-rooms, tinkering to get the last possible ounce of power from their motors, lubricating things or just polishing the brasswork. Some children were employed on washing down the bright paintwork of the cabins or polishing the visible brassware, or cleaning out the cabins, while others had the chance for a game with friends they only saw on such rare occasions.

Jesse found himself recruited to sweep off the length of the long deck, while Luke took a bucket and mop and began to wash down the cabinsides of the *Murray*. He was hard at it, head down over the broom, when Luke suddenly called quietly to him:

'Coom 'ere!' He looked up to see the other boy beckoning him urgently:

'What is it?' Luke gestured with his head at two men who were approaching; men dressed in formal-looking suits. One of them carried a brief-case:

''Ealth h'inspectors!' Jesse put the broom down and walked along the deck to where he was standing; the two men were close enough to hear what they said now. Luke stuck his hand out; surprised, Jesse took it as the older boy said loudly:

'Bye then, Freddie! Thanks for coomin by – we'll see yeh

nex' toime we're this way, eh?' Realising what was expected of him, he shook Luke's hand and replied:

'Yeah – good ter see yeh, Luke. Good luck on the trip!' Luke had leant close as if in friendship, and he whispered in Jesse's ear:

'Keep out o' soight 'til they've gone, roight?'

He turned and walked away, around the nearest building. He hurried around it, and peered around the corner, to see the men stepping aboard the boat, an air of arrogance about them. Mrs Kain was hurrying across to join them, and followed them as they squeezed into the cabin. It looked as if they would be a little while, so he went for a stroll around the area, looking around the complex of buildings, following the two pairs of duplicated locks to where they opened into a big basin, which was itself joined through a bigger lock into what looked like a wide river. A boatman stood there at the point, gazing out across the water; he turned to Jesse:

'Wi' boats?'

'Yeah' the boy replied 'the *Murray.*'

'Ah. Clayton's, roight?'

'Yeah.' The man nodded out at the waterway before them:

'Yeh're their noo kid, eh? That there's the ship canal – yeh'll be goin' out there termorrer, be'ind the tug. You tek care out there, boy, 'old on toight.'

'Is it dangerous?' The water looked placid, for all its great extent.

'Can be, boy. Moy oldest boy was drownded out there, two year ago, washed off the boat when a big ship coom by. So you tek care, eh?'

'I will!' The man smiled at him and turned away; Jesse, struck by his tragedy, called after him: 'I'm really sorry!' The man raised a hand in acknowledgement but kept on walking.

Jesse made his way back up to the boats, in time to see the two men leaving the *Murray* and heading for Abel Beechey's pair. He slipped up to Mrs Kain, who was standing with a relieved but annoyed look on her face:

'Everythin' all right?' he asked; she smiled at him:

'Yeah, foine, Jesse. Yeh'd better get down insoide, 'case they sees yeh.' He nodded and climbed aboard, ducked down into the cabin. She went back to her washing; Jesse found Luke inside, tidying up:

'What was that all about?' Luke looked up:

'Oi tol' yeh – 'ealth h'inspectors. They coom 'ere all the toime.'

'Oh. Is everythin' okay?'

'Yeah, they didn' find mooch ter complain 'bout this toime. Joost the cracked flue on the fore-cabin chimbley, 'n they let oos off wi' that when Mam tol' 'em the boat's bein' docked after ar nex' trip any'ow.'

'Oh – right.' Luke actually smiled at him then:

'Yeh did well, pickin' oop what Oi was gettin' at.' Jesse smiled back:

'Yeah – well, I gathered what yeh wanted me ter do. We fooled 'em, eh?'

'S'roight. Tol' 'em yeh was moy cousin, from 'ere in the town.'

'They believed yeh?'

'Yeah – well, mebbe not, but they can' prove ootherwoise, can they?'

'Luke – yeh could've got shot of me again, couldn' yeh?'

'Yeah – missed me chance, eh? But loike Oi tol' yeh afore, we don' do nothin' ter 'elp the 'thorities on the bank, roight?'

'Yeah – right. Thanks, anyway.' Luke shrugged his shoulders and turned back to his task, and Jesse sat down on the step to keep out of his way. The older boy turned his head:

''Ow 'bout gettin' oos all soom bread 'n cheese, eh? Mam'll do dinner fer later terday, as we're toied oop.'

Jesse did as he suggested; Mrs Kain took a break from her labours to brew a fresh pot of tea for them all, and called the two girls from their play with the other children. Then she coerced Luke into lending Jesse some spare clothes so that she could wash his. The coloured boy had only what he stood up in; she insisted on having his underclothes as well, leaving him alone in the cabin to strip and dress in Luke's spares.

The chores and chatter continued through the rest of the afternoon; dinner was taken around tea-time, and the children were all packed off to bed early for once. Despite their protests, that included Rosie and Alice, their mother quietly insistent. Once they were settled, she and Luke strolled over to the Canal Tavern, just back by the last bridge they'd come under; after a little thought, she took Jesse along too, not wanting to leave him alone – he sat in a corner, with a glass of lemonade and a packet of crisps, enjoying the sometimes-rowdy banter of the boaters in the crowded bar-room, tapping his feet to the rhythm when someone began to play a melodeon or strum a banjo and joining in the singing when he could pick up the words.

Then they were back to the boats, settled for sleep themselves quite early, ready for an equally-early start in the morning.

Jesse was awakened in the pre-dawn twilight by the explosive 'Boof!... Tonk... Tonk.. Tonk-Tonk-Tonk-Tonk' of an engine starting up. Luke was already out of bed and hurriedly dressing; Jesse waited until he clambered out of the cabin to rise himself and quickly draw on his freshly-laundered shirt and trousers, pull on his boots and throw on his coat. A quick mug of tea, and they were on the move:

'We wants ter get the first tug, or we'll be waitin' 'ere all day' Mrs Kain informed him: 'We bow-'auls the boat down 'ere – Prince can 'ave a rest 'til we gets back later.' They followed the Beecheys with their pair of boats down the two narrow locks, and then through the last big lock into the bottom basin. There the three boats were picked up and tied behind a big, powerful-looking tug, the *Murray* between the sterns of the *Stour* and the *Hudson*. The tug driver didn't seem inclined to hang around – they were out of the basin and storming along the wide expanse of the Ship Canal in no time at all. After the slow travel of the previous days, they seemed to Jesse to be flying, a bow-wave creaming away each side of the boat's stem-post. In what felt like no time at all, they were being manoeuvred into place alongside a wide wharf, covered in pipes and valves, and tied securely against the edge. The two other boats were breasted on outside of them, and then men were swarming across all three with heavy flexible hoses, lifting the hatches cut into the boats' decks and feeding them inside.

Valves were opened, and the thick smell of oil permeated the air as it was pumped, ton after ton, into each of the boats. Behind them, moored to another part of the same wharf, a coastal tanker dwarfed the canal boats which had seemed so big and long to Jesse. Before long, all three were settling deeper into the water; and then, more rushing and bustle as the hoses were removed. Each boat's crew made a careful job of closing the hatches and securing them tightly; Jesse was careful to watch exactly how Luke went about it, and to copy him, making sure the hatches he closed were completely water-tight.

And then the tug was back, now taking the other pair on a long tow-line. Luke threw their own line to Mr Beechey, who fastened it to the stern of his own boat; the tug drew away, hauling the pair off first, and then the *Murray,* on its own. A wide sweeping turn, and they were away, back towards the basin and locks of Ellesmere Port. The journey now was quite frightening, or so Jesse thought – the boat was so deep in the water that it seemed the wash would come pouring over its bows at any moment. But the tug driver kept going, maybe a little slower than he had when they were still empty; and they stayed afloat despite Jesse's fears. And approaching the turn into the basin, his attention was distracted by the sight of another sea-going ship, steaming past them, headed upstream the way they had come.

The tug driver ignored the immense vessel, towering over them like a steel cliff, and swung his boat into the basin's entrance. Mr Beechey's pair followed it; and Luke heaved his tiller over to do the same. Just at that moment, the rolling wash of the freighter hit the side of the *Murray,* and it gave a sharp, lurching roll to one side, and then snapped back the other way with equal suddenness. Jesse, standing on the forward part of the deck, grabbed the mast to stop himself being thrown overboard. He heard a shriek from behind him; and Luke's yell:

'ROSIE!' Jesse looked around; Luke was staring, and beside him in the stern well, Mrs Kain had a look of horror on her face. He didn't need to be told – the other boatman's tale of tragedy came home to him with awful force as he realised the little girl had disappeared.

Chapter Fourteen

A moment of stunned incomprehension in which no-one could move, broken by the terrified screams of the nine-year-old in the heaving water.

'ROSIE!' Mrs Kain's voice held fear and desperation. Luke seemed rooted to the spot; Jesse had no time for thought – he threw off his coat, kicked off his boots, and dived over the side of the boat. He knew roughly where Rosie was from the direction of her screams; he struck out towards her, ploughing through the rolling waves of the freighter's wash. But he couldn't see where she was; struggling to keep himself afloat in the rough water, swept along in the tumbling wash from the big ship, he began to regret his impulsive action. And then a rising panic gripped him as he was swept under, a terror that he was going to die the same way as the other boatman's son: *I ain't going ter make this!* He struggled for air, losing any idea of which way was up as he was rolled over and over, until a sorrowful resignation began to take over, dulling his senses from the lack of oxygen: *Is this how it all ends…?*

But then the waves began to subside, and suddenly his head broke the surface; he gulped down several frantic breaths, and then he was back in control, no longer staring death in the face. And there she was! An arm waving frantically, her voice stilled now – but he could see her. He swam to her, put his arm round her shoulders and spoke to her to calm her terror:

'Rosie! Rosie! It's okay, I'm 'ere!' Her panic eased, and she threw her arms round his neck.

'Hey – not so tight! 'Ang on, let's get out of 'ere.'

He began to swim, struggling with the child in his arms – but it was, thankfully, only a matter of yards now to the bank. A steel ladder was set into the concrete edge by the entrance to the basin, and he made for that. As they drew closer, a man appeared at the top and climbed down, reaching out – Jesse thrust the little girl into his grasp, and hung on while he half-helped, half-carried her up onto the top. Then he climbed out, and hauled himself slowly up until he stood on the side, water streaming out of his clothes.

Rosie lay on the concrete, in a puddle of water, choking and coughing, the man kneeling at her side. Her eyes opened, and sought Jesse's, and the look in them said more than words. And then her mother was there, kneeling, rubbing her hands:

'Rosie! Oh, Rosie, Oi thought we'd lost yeh...' She looked around: 'Jesse...' She leapt to her feet and grabbed the boy into a bear-hug: 'Oh Jesse! You brave, brave boy! Thank God yeh were there...' Then she turned back to her daughter and bent to pick the child up: 'Let's get you in the warm, Rosie, get those wet clothes off of yeh...'

Alice and Luke were both there – the girl flashed a look of gratitude at Jesse and hurried after her mother, to where the *Murray* was tied at the side of the basin. Luke drew a deep breath, looking very uncomfortable; then he held out his hand to Jesse:

'Thank yeh. We owe yeh – *Oi* owes yeh, fer what yeh joost did. Loike Mam said, thank God yeh were there.' Jesse shook his head:

'You'd 'ave saved 'er if I 'adn't got there first.' Luke gave a sad little chuckle:

'Nah Oi wouldn't! Oi can' swim – none of oos can.'

'Whyever not?' Jesse was astonished.

'Oi s'pose we don' 'ave the toime ter learn, any more'n we gets ter go ter school. 'N we does ar best not ter fall in, any'ow.'

Jesse took the proffered hand, and the two boys shook solemnly:

'Coom on, we'd best see 'ow Mam's gettin' on wi' littl'un.' Luke turned away with the first genuine smile he'd given the younger boy; Jesse went to follow, but the man took him by the arm. He looked up, and realised it was the same boatman he'd met the day before. The look on his face was unfathomable:

'That was the bravest thing Oi've seen, boy. Yeh could've drownded, yerself.' Jesse smiled:

'I thought I was goin' to, fer a while!' The man took his hand and shook it vigorously, and Jesse felt a surge of sadness for him: 'I wish – someone could've done the same fer your son.'

The man just nodded, and patted him on the shoulder as he turned away.

In the boat cabin, Mrs Kain had stripped the little girl of her wet clothes and was energetically towelling her down when Jesse looked in. Alice had sorted out fresh clothing for her; now, she beckoned him inside:

'Get yerself in 'ere, Jesse! Luke!' She called to her brother, standing outside: 'Go 'n foind some droy things fer Jesse!' Booted footsteps hurried away to the fore-cabin as he climbed damply down the steps. Mrs Kain handed him the towel and began to help Rosie getting dressed again:

'Get them things off yeh – Luke'll be back wi' droy stuff in a mo.' He looked at Alice, who giggled:

'Oi've seen boys wi' no clothes on before! T'ain't the toime ter be shy, yeh'll catch yer death!' He hesitated, but then, with a mental shrug of the shoulders, began to undress. He covered himself with the towel as quickly as he could, and began to feel more comfortable as he rubbed himself down. Then Luke was at the hatches, handing down a pile of dry clothes; he dressed again, gratefully, aware of Alice's amused gaze from where she sat within her mother's bed-hole.

'We oughta be gettin' ahead' Luke suggested carefully; his mother nodded, but her words disagreed:

'Give oos a minute or two, boy! Oi'll stoke oop the range ter droy these two out 'n mek oos all a mug o' soup, then we'll get away.'

'Roight-o, Mam. Oi'll go fer Prince.' He strode away, and Mrs Kain opened the fire-hole door and riddled the glowing coals within, lifted the stewpot onto the top and began to stir its contents. A couple of minutes later, she ladled out two mugs, and handed them to Rosie and Jesse:

'There yeh go, get that down yeh both. 'N you stay 'ere – Luke 'n Alice 'n me can get the boat oop the locks, roight? You stay 'n get warm.' She looked at Jesse: ''Ow can Oi ever thank you, lad? If it weren't fer you...' He just shrugged, and smiled at her, embarrassed by her gratitude; she pulled him in to an embrace and kissed his cheek. Then, holding him at arm's length, she smiled tenderly into his eyes, marvelling as the sunlight through the doors gave them a deep bronze glow. She turned and climbed out of the cabin; Alice stood up:

'Jesse?' He turned to see tears in her eyes; she opened her mouth to speak, but then just threw her arms around him: 'Thank you! Thank yeh so mooch...' He felt another kiss on his cheek; and then she was gone, hurrying after her mother.

The boat bumped against the side, and then began to move as Prince pulled it towards the first of the locks. Jesse sat down beside Rosie on the side-bed; the little girl hadn't spoken since he entered the cabin, and seemed to be still in shock after her ordeal. Now she looked up at him with a shy smile which reminded him rather of her sister; and then she was on his lap, holding him tightly, her head on his shoulder, crying quietly. Rather nonplussed, he put his arms around her, patted her gently on the back:

'It's okay Rosie, yeh're safe 'n warm now...'

Chapter Fifteen

Jesse lost track of time for a while. The boat bumped and rocked from time to time, and water rustled past the hull; quiet voices sounded through the open slide hatch now and again, and he was aware of the subdued bustle outside as Mrs Kain and her son and daughter worked up the locks. He sat there for somewhere between no time and forever, holding the little girl whose storm of tears quickly passed, holding her as she lay against him, her arms clasped tightly around his neck, her head on his shoulder. She seemed almost to be asleep, so motionless was she; feeling the gentle movement of her breathing, he felt a deep fondness for the child, and a thankfulness that she had survived such a close brush with death. That her survival had been due to his own efforts seemed unimportant, inconsequential.

With time to reflect upon his situation, he began to realise that he had grown just as fond of the buxom, jovial boatwoman; and his feelings for her older daughter were edging towards something deeper. And with that realisation a sense of sadness overtook him – only a few more days, two or three at the most, and they would be back in Birmingham, and he would be on his own again, left to fend for himself as best he could in the strange, dark city. How would he fare? Could he find some kind of work, would anyone take on a kid of thirteen? He'd have to lie about his age – being tall, he could pass for fourteen, maybe even fifteen if he was lucky. And where would he live? Back on the streets? All the time, the police would be looking for him; and if they caught him, he'd be back in care, and in trouble for the money he'd 'borrowed' when he ran away.

If only... Life here on the boat seemed so easy, so simple, by comparison. Even working the locks wasn't really so hard – he wasn't afraid of exercise, he could cope with anything he'd seen so far. Maybe... But no – Luke would never accept him, he'd made that very plain. And even Jesse had to admit that he was right when he said that they didn't need anyone else, the four of them were more than capable of managing the boat and the horse on their own. So there was no choice – and he had to stay around Birmingham, because how would his father find him if he went anywhere else?

Despair rising in his heart, he gave vent to a long, deep sigh. Rosie stirred in his arms and lifted her head; blinking her eyes, she smiled at him:

'Jesse...'

'Sssh, it's all right, Rosie.'

'You saved my loife...'

'Sssh, it's not important. All that matters is yeh're all right.' She smiled into his eyes for a moment before stretching her neck to kiss his cheek, and then settled again, snuggling down into his arms and resting her head against his chest.

A little while later, the cabin doors opened and Mrs Kain stepped down to join them, sitting on the coal-box as she slipped the beret from her head:

''Ow are you two feelin'? Better now?' Rosie let go her hold on Jesse and turned to her mother:

'Yes, Mam. Oi'm h'okay now.'

'Good girl. It's a lovely day out there, whoy don' you go 'n sit in the sunshoine fer a whoile?'

'Yes, Mam. Mam – can Oi 'ave a cuppa tea?'

''Course yeh can – you go on outsoide 'n Oi'll bring yeh one.'

Rosie got up and, with a last smile over her shoulder for Jesse, climbed out of the cabin. Mrs Kain picked up the kettle and weighed it in her hand before turning and handing it out through the doors:

'Put oos some water in there, Alice.' Moments later it was handed back in, and she fussed around, placing it on the range and riddling the fire. At last, she turned around, and sat beside Jesse on the sidebed. She looked at him, a gentle smile on her face:

'Jesse – 'Ow can Oi ever thank you...' He interrupted her:

'Please, Missus Kain, I... Don't make a big fuss, please? I only...'

'You only saved moy little girl's loife, Jesse.' She spoke softly now: 'Nothin' can ever repay that, 'n "thank you" don't seem ter cover it. Oi don' know what else ter say, lad.'

'Then don' say nothin'!' He smiled back at her: 'I'm just 'appy that Rosie's okay, right?'

'All roight, lad.' She hesitated: 'That man as 'elped yeh with 'er, on the steps?'

'Yeah?'

''Is name's Charlie Bingham; 'e used ter be on the boats, loike oos. 'E give it oop, after 'is son was drownded – 'e went in the river back there, joost loike Rosie. 'E works at the Port, now.'

'Yeah – 'e tol' me 'bout it.' Jesse quickly changed the subject: 'Where are we?'

'On the way back ter Chester. We'll still be oop Northgate ternoight with a bit o' luck, back where we stopped on the way down.' She looked up as the kettle began to boil, and reached over to brew the tea. Five mugs soon steamed on the lowered table-cupboard, and she handed one to Jesse:

'There yeh go – are yeh coomin' out in the sun with the rest of oos?' He nodded, and picked up another mug to follow her up the steps into the daylight. Alice took her tea from him as he gazed around in the evening sunshine, smiling to himself as he saw the washing-line strung from mast to cabin with his own and Rosie's clothes drying on it; Rosie turned from her perch on the cabin-top and reached for the mug her mother held out to her.

'Luke – tea!' The teenager ran back at her shout, grabbed his mug and hurried forward again to catch up with the horse. Prince had, as usual, continued plodding steadily on all the while, and it occurred now to Jesse to ask:

'Why does someone always follow the 'orse? I mean, 'e keeps goin' on 'is own, don't 'e?' Mrs Kain laughed, but it was Alice who replied:

''E does fer a whoile, but sooner or later 'e notices there's no-one there, 'n then 'e slows roight down! 'E'd prob'ly stop altergether if we let 'im.'

Dusk was gathering as they approached the outskirts of Chester once more. Mrs Kain had returned to the cabin, leaving the youngsters in the fresh air, to prepare their dinner, and soon an appetising aroma of stewing mutton drifted out to their nostrils. As the boat passed under the last small bridge below the massive staircase of Northgate Locks, its accompanying railway viaduct looming a hundred yards in front of them, she put her head out of the hatches:

'We'll stop 'ere fer ternoight, by the yard. Dinner's 'bout ready, 'n we've all 'ad a bit of a day, eh?' She raised her voice: 'Luke! Stoppin' 'ere, roight?'

The boy looked around and raised an arm in acknowledgement, slowing Prince to a halt on the towpath. The boat drifted in against the bank under Alice's guiding hand, and Jesse stood up to step off with the stern rope as he'd seen the others do previously, getting an approving smile from the boatwoman as he did so.

With the *Murray* safely tied up for the night, Luke led the horse over the bridge to the boatyard and stables opposite, while Mrs Kain ladled out five helpings of stew and placed a baked potato with each. As usual, the two girls sat at the table in the cabin to eat; Jesse took his plate gratefully and sat on the edge of the well-deck. Luke came back to join them, and sat opposite him, to eat in a taciturn silence – but more than once, Jesse caught him staring across with a thoughtful, almost puzzled, look on his face.

More tea followed their food, and the boatwoman leant in the hatches to drink hers:

'We're gettin' short o' stuff. Jesse – will yeh go wi' h'Alice in the mornin', ter the shops? Yeh can get the bus ter Christleton 'n we'll meet yeh there, she'll show yeh where. Yeh 'ear that, Alice?' She called back down the steps, and an answering 'Yes, Mam' echoed back.

'Roight then – ter bed, all of yeh! Oop sharp in the mornin'!'

* * *

Matt Whelan had been a policeman for nearly twenty years. Born and raised in Ellesmere Port, he'd risen to the rank of sergeant, but had little ambition to go further – he enjoyed the life he had, and really didn't want any more responsibility. Off duty that night, he wandered around to the Grosvenor, the little pub a couple of streets away from the terraced house where he lived with his wife and two children. He was just raising his first pint when a familiar voice sounded behind him:

'Don' put yer wallet away yet, there's anoother thirst 'ere mate!' He looked around:

'Charlie! What'll yeh have, mate?'

'Pint o' the usual, Matt, thanks.'

Each with a glass in his hand, the policeman and the ex-boater perched on stools by the bar.

'Off duty, Matt?'

'Yeah. Been on all weekend, got a coupl'a days off now.'

'Roight.' Bingham took a long swig of his beer: 'Eh, yeh missed soomat oop the Port terday, mate!'

'Oh ah?'

'Aye. Little girl got tipped off 'er boat inter the ship canal, joost as they were coomin' back ter the basin.'

'Oh no!' Whelan knew all about his companion's tragedy, and a wave of horror swept over him: 'Is she...?' But Bingham laughed:

'She's h'okay! There was anoother kid on the boat, jumped in 'n saved 'er. Nigh on got drownded 'imself, mind, doin' it.'

'Oh, thank goodness! 'Er brother, was it?'

'Nah. Dunno 'oo 'e was, with 'em joost fer a roide, Oi reckon. Black kid, Gawd knows where 'e'd coom from.'

'A black lad?' Bells were ringing in the policeman's mind: 'On a boat?'

'Yeah. Clayton's 'orse-boat, the *Moorray.*'

'Ah – 'ow old was this kid?'

'Dunno – 'bout fourteen, mebbe.'

'Ah...'

'Brave kid, though. Risked 'is own loife ter save little Rosie – Annie Kain's kiddie.'

'Yeah – I know the family...' But Whelan's tone was thoughtful.

Chapter Sixteen

Jesse stood once more in that huge, darkly oppressive room, surrounded by hostile faces. One of them loomed over him, bewigged, a scarlet cloak about its shoulders:

'You stole two pounds and ten shillings! You've got to go to prison!'

'No! No – I only borrowed it – I had to!'

'You never had to steal, that's a lie! No-one has to steal! You're just like your father!'

'No – no – no...'

'Hey!'

Jesse came to, hot and sweaty under his blanket, and forced his eyes open.

'Hey – stop shoutin' will yeh!' He looked blearily around:

'Nnnh – sorry...'

'Woke me oop wi' yer bellowin', yeh did.' Luke sounded annoyed. Jesse rubbed his eyes:'Sorry – I was dreamin'. I didn' mean ter!'

'Yeah, well.' Luke sighed: 'Moight as well get oop any'ow, Oi s'pose. It's gettin' loight out there.' He swung his feet to the floor: 'What was yeh dreamin' about?'

'I drempt they caught me. They was sendin' me ter prison fer takin' the money.'

'Huh! What d'yeh h'expect? Ruddy stoopid thing ter do! If yeh'd joost roon away they wouldn' bother so mooch.'

'Yeah, I know. But 'ow was I goin' ter manage, eh?' Luke just shrugged his shoulders as he pulled on his trousers:

'That's your lookout. Yeh could've stayed where yeh were.'

'No I couldn'! 'E was – knockin' me abaht, treatin' me like a ruddy slave. I couldn' stay there, could I?' There was a hint of sympathy now in the look the older boy gave him, but his words were indifferent:

'Dunno. T'ain't moy concern, any'ow.' Luke dragged on his coat, stuck his cap on his head and climbed out of the cabin, thrusting back the slide-hatch.

Jesse heaved a sigh himself now. Despite what had happened the day before, Luke still hadn't changed his opinion of him, still didn't want him around. He slipped the blanket from his shoulders, lowered his feet to the floor and reached for his shirt.

Out in the cold light of the dawn, Luke was hurriedly mopping the dew from the sides of the cabin. He looked around as Jesse emerged:

'Tek the water-can 'n fill it oop will yeh? There's a tap over on the yard, 'cross the bridge.'

Jesse hefted the nearly-empty can from the roof and carried it across. It took him a minute or two to find the tap; then he filled the can to the brim, closed the hinged flap over it and set off back. Three gallons of water was surprisingly heavy – he wondered how the little girl ever managed to lift it, never mind heave it up onto the cabin they way she did. Back at the boat, he struggled to do the same, despite the fact that the cabin roof was about three feet closer to the water now, with a full load in the oil-tanks.

The smell of fresh tea reached his nostrils as the hatch slid open; Mrs Kain emerged with a grin:

'Tea, boys! Bread 'n cheese coomin' oop.' Moments later, he was munching gratefully. The girls had gone for the horse, having eaten already, and Luke was checking over the boat ready for a full day's travel, setting the towrope in place on the foredeck.

'You h'okay, Jesse?' Mrs Kain had noted his quietness.

'Yeah, I'm fine thanks.' She was still looking at him, and he felt he had to say something more: 'I didn' sleep very well, las' night.'

'Ah – roight. S'long as yeh're all roight, lad?'

'I'll be fine, really!' She nodded and ducked back in to the cabin, emerging moments later with a dark brown tweed cap in her hand:

''At fer yeh, boy. It were moy man's spare one, 'e'd 'ardly wore it.' Jesse took it and slipped it on his head – not a bad fit!

'Thank yeh!'

'Aye – keep it, it suits yeh!' She smiled at him, and he grinned back.

'You want me ter go ter the shops with Alice?'

'Once we're oop Northgate Riser, yes. We needs a bit o' stuff, 'n you can 'elp 'er carry it back, if yeh don' moind?'

'I don' mind at all. It'll be a change.' She gave him a wide smile:

'Yeh're a good boy, Jesse.' He smiled back, but the aftermath of his dream was still in his mind: *It'd be nice if everyone thought that!*

The chatter of the two girls reached his ears as they returned, leading Prince over the bridge. Finishing his tea, he tucked the windlass in his belt and followed Luke as he walked ahead to set the first lock. Seen from below, Northgate locks were even more daunting, seeming to tower above him in the half-light of their deep rock-sided cutting to an impossibly-distant sky above.

'Soomthin' special, ain't they?' For once, Luke seemed to sense and almost agree with his feeling of wonder, and he looked around to see an amused light in the older boy's eyes: 'Coom on, let's get on wi' it.'

Jesse's amazement at the astonishing engineering of the three staircase locks persisted as they worked the boat up through them. Looking down into each chamber it seemed impossibly far below them as Mrs Kain deftly steered it through, and there was something majestic about its slow rise to meet them upon the swirling turbulence of the water. After half an hour, it finally rose into the brightening daylight, under the shadow of Chester's towering city walls. Rosie, seemingly fully recovered from her ordeal now, took up her station at Prince's heels as Luke slotted the tiller into place; Mrs Kain despatched her other daughter to the shops, handing over a few shillings in change:

'We needs two tins o' milk, flour fer bread-makin', 'n if the butcher's got some cheap meat, pork or mutton mebbe, we can 'ave it fer dinner ternoight. You knows where to get the bus?'

'Yes, Mam. Coom on, Jesse!' She led him back down the side of the massive locks, and then away into the narrow streets: 'There's a coupl'a shops 'ere knows the boaters, 'n they look after oos, give oos a bit h'extra, loike, fer ar money. They even gives oos stuff on tick, if we're short, 'n we pays fer it nex' toime we're by.'

He tagged along, happy in her company, as she went from shop to shop, cheerfully and efficiently gathering the items her mother had asked for. The shop-keepers all seemed friendly, and he noted how the butcher in particular weighed out the portion she wanted, and then quietly slipped a good handful more of the diced mutton into the bag he handed over. Alice rewarded him with a big smile and a cheerful 'Thank you'.

They passed a newsagents, and he glanced inside:

'Alice – do yeh like choc'late?'

'Ooh yes! But we can't afford it, not often.' He grinned at her:

'Wait 'ere.' In moments he was back, and slipped four thre'penny bars of milk chocolate into her bag.

'Jesse! Yeh shouldn' do that!'

'Why not? I can treat yeh if I want, can' I?'

'You shouldn't...' But the look on her face made his heart sing.

Alice led him towards the centre of the town where they caught a bus, paying the fares with the last of her mother's money. She scampered happily up onto the top deck, and they sat together, gazing out at the city as it rattled its way along.

'Where are we goin'?' He asked.

'Christleton, we meets the boat there. It's a little place, a bit outsoide the town. There's an old wharf there, with a big pub besoide it.'

'Oh – yeah... I think I remember it, on the way up 'ere.' Alice gave him a puzzled look:

'Oop?'

'Yeah – Up North, ain't we? North from Birmingham, right?'

'*Oop* North? Is that what folks on the bank say?'

'Yeah, o' course!' He didn't understand what was so amusing to her; she giggled suddenly, and took his arm in hers:

'On the boats, we says *down* the North!' Now it was his turn to be puzzled:

'Whatever does that mean? How can it be *down?*' Alice laughed again:

'O' course it's down! It's down'ill all the way, silly!' He frowned in perplexity; but then the penny dropped – all the locks had been downhill, since they'd started, and now they were going uphill to get back to Birmingham. Even so, the idea of saying 'down' for going North still seemed all wrong – but he hid his confusion and laughed with her:

'Yeah, okay, I see what yeh mean!'

They got off the bus a little way from a cross-roads, where a pub called the Old Trooper stood on one corner. Alice led him along, over the side-road and past the pub:

'The wharf's joost oop 'ere, we can get 'cross it ter the cut.' But Jesse suddenly hung back, his brow furrowed: A black Wolseley saloon stood at the side of the road, and he didn't need the shiny bell on its bumper or the sign on its roof to recognise a police car. He turned to Alice:

'Where that car is?' She looked:

'Yeah, that's right! Oh – Jesse?'

'Yeah. They're lookin' fer me, 'cos I ran away. If they catches me, they'll send me back, mebbe ter prison even.'

'Prison? Joost fer runnin' away?' He bit his lip:

'No – I... I took some money, too. Just ter keep me goin', like.'

'Oh, Jesse!' He turned away from the hurt in her eyes, but looked back as she said: 'You wouldn' 'ave done that if yeh didn' 'ave ter, Oi knows. But they mustn't catch yeh!' She took the bag he was carrying: 'You keep out o' soight! Wait 'til they're gone – if the boat ain't there, this road goes on close ter the cut fer a bit – catch oop with oos when yeh can.'

'Okay – thanks, Alice!' Impulsively, he grabbed her shoulders and leant forward to kiss her on the cheek.

'Get away! Get out o' soight, Jesse!' But there was a happy smile on her face as she waved him away. He ducked back around the pub and down the side-road as she walked on towards the old wharf.

Chapter Seventeen

Jesse's mind was in turmoil as he paused, just around the corner and out of sight. Why were the police *here?* They couldn't have known that he and Alice were to meet the boat here – so why? And why had they suddenly put in an appearance again? He'd thought, hoped, that after the way Luke had put them off at Market Drayton, they'd given up thinking he was still on the canal. It was all puzzling – and worrying.

Then it occurred to him – maybe they weren't after him at all! They were probably here for some reason that was nothing to do with him. He was running scared, frightened that every copper in the country was on the lookout for him, when they probably had much better things to be doing. But – could he take that risk? What if they *were* looking for him, what if they'd somehow learnt that he *was* still on the boat? No, he'd better do as Alice had said, keep out of the way and try and catch up with them later.

He looked around – the side-road in front of him rose to cross a bridge, and he realised that the canal lay underneath. He walked carefully forward until he could see around the back of the pub building and over the parapet of the bridge. A little way along, he could see the wharf, looking abandoned and derelict; and there were two uniformed figures standing there! It was still possible that the policemen weren't looking for him; they *might* be there for some other reason, even just stopped for break and wandered over to the waterside for no reason at all. But he knew in his heart that wasn't so – they were waiting for the boat, waiting for *him!* The *Murray* was nowhere in sight; but at that moment, the slight form of Alice appeared, bags in hand, on the towpath. He watched as she spoke to the coppers, surprise evident in her body language – *good girl!*

He heard something from behind him, in the distance, and turned around. There was the boat! Maybe a hundred yards away, he could see a lock, and there stood Prince, placidly waiting while it rose into sight over the gate. He watched Luke push the gate open, saw Rosie jump onto the boat as it began to move and the cosy round figure of Mrs Kain at the tiller, and had to fight down the impulse to run down and join them. Instead, he withdrew out of sight again: *Best if they don't know where I am!* He didn't want to put them in a difficult position, having to lie for him – and if truth be told he didn't entirely trust Luke not to give him away, even if he had helped to hide him up to now.

Out of sight in the pub's backyard, he heard the clop – clop – clop as Prince plodded steadily by, scant yards away from him, and then the subdued voices of the boatwoman and her daughter from the stern of the boat. Then came Luke's voice, from the wharf:

'Whoa, Prince, 'old oop there!'

Jesse stole silently out of the yard and back to the bridge, where he peered carfully over the parapet. Alice had stepped onto the deck, and she and Luke were deep in conversation with the two policemen; Mrs Kain got out of the stern well and went up to them as well. They were too far away for him to hear what was said, and his nerves were at breaking point as he watched them talking. Luke gestured back towards the town, and his mother was nodding her head as if to confirm what he was saying. Then one of the coppers was speaking; he nodded too, and then shook hands with them both before turning away. Relief flooded over Jesse – they hadn't given him away, and it looked as if the police weren't sure where he was, if they were letting the boat go on its way. That much was immediately confirmed when Luke whistled Prince into motion again.

Keeping his head down, he turned his attention to the main road where it passed the cross-roads; and moments later, the police car swept past, heading back towards Chester. Looking up again, Jesse saw the boat just disappearing from sight under another bridge. Back in the pub yard, stepping up with the aid of a rubbish bin, he jumped over the back wall and hurried after them.

Despite striding out as fast as he could, he was surprised how long it took him to overtake the boat. But he didn't risk running, remembering the warnings he'd received; and before too long he was within earshot, and called out:

'Missus Kain! Rosie! Wait fer me!' Two heads turned, and he saw them both break into smiles when they saw him. Luke looked back too, and slowed the horse's pace for a moment to allow him to catch up. Mrs Kain steered the stern in close to the bank, and he scrambled over into the well, holding the hand she proffered to help him.

'Thank you!' He was breathless but happy to be back on board; Alice smiled up at him from within the cabin, and Rosie gave him a quick hug.

'Are you all roight, boy?' Mrs Kain asked; he nodded:

'Yes, thanks. Out of breath, that's all. I'm sorry about that...'

'Yes... We need ter talk, boy, but it'll keep fer later.' There was a new sternness in the boatwoman's manner; but then she smiled at him: 'It's good ter see yeh safe, lad. Now – soup all round, eh?' There was a chorus of 'yes, please!' and she ducked down into the cabin, leaving Rosie to steer.

Alice finished putting the shopping away, and then came back out of the cabin to leave room for her mother to turn the remnants of last night's stew into a hot, tasty soup. Jesse grinned at her, and she smiled shyly back:

'Oi've put the choc'late in the larder to keep cool – we'll 'ave it fer supper later, eh?'

'Choc'late?' Rosie's ears perked up, and her sister laughed:

'Jesse got oos a bar each, from the paper-shop!'

'Ooh! Thank yeh, Jesse!' The light in the little girl's eyes made him laugh with sheer pleasure:

'Yeh're welcome, Rosie!'

All three fell silent, and Jesse knew they were thinking about what had happened at the old wharf with the police – but neither girl seemed eager to talk about it. After a few minutes, he could contain his nerves no longer:

'Well – what 'appened back there?' Rosie looked at her sister, while Alice avoided his eyes. At last she turned to him:

'We told 'em yeh were still at the Port. Luke said as we'd brung yeh there 'cos yeh wanted ter get away from Birnigum, 'n then we'd left yeh there.'

'What did yer Mum say?'

'She backed 'im oop, said as that was roight. She – they told 'er what yeh'd done, tekin' that money. Oi'm sorry, Jesse!'

'Yeah – well, I suppose they would, wouldn' they?' His voice was heavy with resignation: 'What did she say 'bout that?'

'She didn' say nothin'. She wants ter talk ter you...'

'Yeah, I know. D'yeh think – she'll let me stay wi' you?' He was fearful of being turned off the boat, left somewhere miles from where he needed to be, but Alice gave him another hopeful smile:

'Oi reckon she will – she'd 'ave not let yeh back on, otherwise. We owes yeh fer Rosie's loife, after all.'

'That's roight!' Rosie sounded indignant at the very idea of leaving him behind: 'Oi don' care what else yeh've done! Oi loves yeh any'ow!' He turned startled eyes on the little girl, and then had to catch her as she flung herself into his arms, leaving her sister to grab the tiller.

'Hey! Hey, Rosie, it's all right...' He held her, astonished at her outburst, seeing over her shoulder the huge grin that had appeared on Alice's face. Then all three of them were laughing:

'It'll be all roight, yeh'll see!' Alice sounded confident of the future, but Jesse was still feeling rather nervous of the interview with her mother that was to come.

The silence that fell between them was relaxed and cheerful, as the boat surged on steadily, ploughing a deeper furrow through the water now than when they had been heading north. Alice kept hold of the tiller; Rosie clambered up to sit on the cabin-top, and Jesse perched on the gunwale at the side of the well. They were back in the slowly undulating countryside of the Cheshire plain, open fields all around with only the occasional village, far or near, to break the monotony. Jesse was trying to remember from the journey before:

'There's a way ter go 'fore the next lock, ain't there?'

'S'roight' Alice confirmed: 'Wharton, Beeston Two 'n Tilstone. Then Bunbury Riser. But it's a while 'fore we gets ter the first'n.' She gave him a thoughtful look: 'D'yeh want ter 'ave a go? Steerin', Oi mean.' He stared at her:

'Er – dunno. What would yer Mum say?'

'Oh, Mam won' moind! S'long as yeh does what Oi tells yeh.'

'You sure?'

'Go on boy, 'ave a go!' The boatwoman's voice sounded from down below, and Jesse and Alice exchanged grins:

'All right then! What do I do?' Alice laughed:

'Joost coom 'n stand 'ere, in the 'atches' she made way for him, and he stepped gingerly into the space she'd vacated: 'Now tek 'old o' the 'ellum.' He put his arm over the heavy wooden tiller in imitation of the way he'd seen them all do.

'Now – joost keep yer eye on where yeh're goin', keep the mast loined oop down the middle o' the cut. 'N remember, yeh moves the 'ellum t'other way to where yeh wants ter go. Loike this:' She leant over and pushed the tiller away towards the left of the boat, and he watched the fore-end of the boat begin to swing to the right: 'Now you bring it back. Move the 'ellum ter me – that's roight – 'n back ter the middle – there yeh are!' Jesse felt an unaccustomed pride at the way the big boat responded to his touch, turning back to his left as he moved the tiller the other way, and then coming straight again as he let it swing back to its central postion under its own weight. *Hey, this is easy!* He glanced over to see her smiling broadly at him, and felt the grin spreading over his face. But then her smile became a chuckle:

'Look where yeh're goin'!' Turning back, he realised that that moment's inattention had got them drifting off towards the far bank again, and he hurried to try and straighten their course. But he overdid it, and then they were heading towards the towpath. Close to panic, he heard Alice and Rosie both laughing; and then a hand landed on the tiller next to his, and his tutor gently steered them back on line. He heaved a sigh of relief:

'T'ain't as easy as it looks, is it?' The girls both laughed again, as Alice told him:

'S'easy when yeh gets the 'ang of it. We've both been doin' it since we was little.'

'Yeah – yeh're lucky, you two. I wish...' He broke off, and shrugged, feeling their eyes on him: 'I mean...'

'Oi wish, too.' There was a sad smile on Alice's face as he glanced quickly at her before concentrating on the boat's progress. Embarrassed, he changed the subject:

''Ow 'bout goin' inter the locks? The narrer ones, I mean. I couldn' never do that, not like you do, without even touchin' the sides.'

'Yes yeh could, wi' a bit o' practice!'

'But – yeh've 'ardly got an inch or two ter spare!'

'Oh, t'ain't difficult, not really.'

'Mam won' let me steer inter the locks!' Rosie's voice was raised in protest.

'You spend too mooch toime gazin' at the lambs in the fields 'stead o' watchin' where yeh're goin'!' The voice from below sounded again, and Rosie subsided into a frown.

The late morning sunshine grew warm as they travelled on. Careful to keep his eyes constantly on the canal in front of them and concentrate on what he was doing, Jesse soon learned that he only needed to move the big tiller very gently, through a small arc, to keep the boat moving smoothly along the centre of the channel. And before long he was really enjoying himself, feeling relaxed and proud, and happy in the knowledge that if he did get it wrong, Alice was there to rescue him.

She let him steer for over an hour – Mrs Kain appeared with steaming mugs of soup for them, and gave him an approving look before calling out to Luke to come back for his. Eventually, as the towering landmark of Beeston Castle loomed away to their right, Alice took over again:

'Lock's coomin' oop, Jesse.' He looked around for his windlass, and heard Rosie snigger:

'Where is it – 'ave yeh 'idden it?' Alice joined in the laughter as Rosie told him:

'It's in yer belt!' He felt behind him, and grinned ruefully when he found it, still tucked in there since they'd worked up Northgate first thing that morning.

Now they were climbing further uphill; four big locks in quite quick succession, and then the two-lock staircase of Bunbury, with its semi-derelict stable block at the top. They ate, another of Mrs Kain's delicious stews with fresh crusty bread baked in the little range, on the long level pound that led them back to and past the town of Nantwich. Luke was steering now, so Jesse didn't expect, nor did he get, another go. The sun was sinking towards the west as they worked through the two narrow locks of Hack Green; an hour later and they were approaching the bottom of the Audlem flight.

Working through the first lock, Mrs Kain called them all together:

'Oi knows it's early, but we'll stop 'ere ternoight.'

'Oh, Mam...' Luke went to protest, but she held up her hand:

'We were be'ind when we started, 'n we lost more toime wi' them coppers. There ain't no decent stables past 'ere 'til we gets ter Drayton, 'n that's too far. We'll go oop the four, 'n stop there. Roight?'

'Yes, Mam' three voices chorused.

Chapter Eighteen

It was getting dark by the time they had worked the boat up through the first four locks, into the last of the longer pounds. The morning would see them quickly up the nine locks of the 'thick', and then the last two of the Audlem flight before travelling on to Adderley Locks and Market Drayton. Stopping at Audlem village overnight meant they would be about three hours behind Mrs Kain's usual schedule – but they could still be back and unloaded in two more days. A quick turn-around, and they would be away northwards again on Friday. *Without the laddie,* she reflected as the girls headed off with Prince to bed him down for the night and Luke and Jesse tidied the boat, coiling the ropes and mopping down the cabins. She had grown fond of the boy, too, a feeling not entirely reliant on the debt she owed him for her daughter's life: *Whatever 'e's done, 'e ain't a bad kid...*

Another pair of Clayton's boats had been tied in the pound below, outside the old warehouse by the wharf; Harold Clutton, in the hatches of the *Orwell,* had waved his old pipe with a cheery ''Ow d'yeh do, Annie' as they passed. As Luke stowed the mop against the watercan on the roof, he strolled up to them:

'Yeh coomin' fer an ale, Annie?'

'Not ternoight, 'Arold, Oi got things ter see to. Yeh goin', Luke?'

'D'yeh moind, Mam?'

''Course not – you go 'n h'enjoy yerself. Not too late, moind, we needs ter be away sharpish in the mornin'.'

'Coom on then lad! See yeh soon, Annie.'

Man and boy walked off towards the village, passing the two chattering girls as they returned from the stables. Their mother greeted them cheerily:

'Roight – supper's on the table fer you two. Then bed, h'okay? 'N we'll be oop sharp in the mornin'. Pour a cuppa fer me 'n Jesse, will yeh? Tea's made.'

'Yes, Mam.' Alice sounded disappointed, but she ducked into the cabin, followed by her sister. She reappeared to hand them a mug each, and then retired inside once more. Mrs Kain turned to the brown boy:

'Coom 'n sit 'ere wi' me, Jesse.' He took a seat beside her on the deck, his feet resting on the towpath: 'Now – Oi reckon as it's 'bout toime we 'ad a chat.'

'Yes, Missus Kain.' It was the moment he'd been dreading, but he looked up at her steadily.

'So what 'appened, lad? Whoy did yeh run away loike that?' He averted his eyes:

'Well – arter me Dad went away, they sent me ter live wi' this fam'ly, see? But I don't reckon they really wanted me, except ter do all the work fer 'em. *She* made me do all the chores in the 'ouse, 'n *'e'd* gi' me a beatin' if I 'adn't done it all when 'e got in from work. 'N their son – 'e was older'n me – 'e'd just mek fun o' me, call me nigger 'n jungle-bunny, 'n things like that, 'n 'it me when they weren't lookin'.' She sighed:

'Yeah, Oi can see as yeh'd want ter get out o' that.' She paused expectantly, and Jesse plucked up his courage, knowing that she knew already:

'When I scarpered, one night arter they'd all gone ter bed, I... I took the money 'e'd left lyin' on the sideboard. I didn' 'ave nothin' – 'ow was I goin' ter manage?' He looked up, willing her to understand:

''Ow mooch was it?' He dropped his eyes again:

'Two pound ten.'

'Oi see. Jesse?' He met her gaze: 'Oi do see whoy yeh took it, Oi knows 'ow yeh must 'ave felt. But it were a silly thing ter do, boy.'

'Yeah, I knows that now. Luke said – 'e said that if I'd just run away, they prob'ly wouldn' bother comin' arter me.'

''E's roight too, Jesse. So – what're we goin' ter do wi' yeh, eh?'

'If yeh'll just let me come wi' yeh, back ter Birmingham – I'll tek care o' meself then.'

'Is Birnigum the best place fer yeh ter be? Mebbe we should'a really left yeh at the Port – they'd soon lose h'interest in yeh, so far away.'

'No! I've got to stay 'round, so's my Dad can find me when – when 'e comes back.'

'Ah – now, 'bout yer Pa, Jesse. That copper said as one reason they wanted ter foind yeh was 'cause they didn' want yeh ter end oop loike yer father. What did 'e mean by that, Oi wonder?'

Jesse stared at her, not sure what to say, afraid of the truth but unprepared to lie to her. He took a drink of his tea to cover his confusion, but when he looked back she was still gazing expectantly at him.

'Joost where is yer Pa, Jesse? Really?' He swallowed hard, feeling tears welling up behind his eyes:

''E's... 'E's in prison.' *I ain't goin ter cry!* But in spite of his best efforts the tears spilled over, to run down his cheeks; he looked up in surprise as he felt her comforting arm encircle his shoulders:

'Oi thought as mooch.' Her voice was gentle: 'T'ain't your shame, boy, that's 'is mistake, not your'n. What 'appened?' Jesse tried to collect his thoughts, mopping his eyes with the handkerchief she proffered to him:

'Like I told Alice, 'e's a driver. 'E's a brilliant driver, faster'n anyone! 'E used ter drive racing cars, once. Then 'e went ter sea, on merchant ships, 'n met my Mum in Jamaica. When 'e come 'ome with 'er, some gangsters persuaded 'im ter drive fer them. I dunno why 'e did it – I s'pose it were easy money. 'E'd get a car, fix it up so's it'd go faster, 'n then they'd do a bank or summat, 'n 'e'd drive them away, too quick fer the police ter catch 'em.' He paused for breath – now he'd started, the need to tell her had becoming overwhelming:

'Then, las' year, it all went wrong. The gang got caught, but 'e escaped – they was inside a jeweller's, but 'e was out in the car. So we come ter Birmingham, to get away from the cops, 'n 'e started drivin' fer a gang up there. But then they all got caught, 'im 'n all...' He drew a shuddering breath: ''E got four years. The judge said as they'd let 'im orf light, 'cause 'e 'adn't been in the shop threatenin' people. The others got eight years each! 'Is lawyer said as 'e might get out arter three, if 'e be'aves 'imself...'

At last it was out. Jesse felt drained, but at the same time strangely relieved, as if telling her had lifted some of the weight from his own shoulders. The boatwoman didn't speak for a while but held him close, and he let his head rest against her ample shoulder until she asked:

''Ave yeh seen 'im since?' He shook his head:

'They won' let me in ter see 'im, 'cause I'm only a kid. They said as I ought ter go ter these other folks, go ter school 'n get on wi' me own life...'

'Aah... Well, we'll 'ave ter see what's ter be done ter get yeh out of all this.' He raised his head:

'Can I stay wi' you? Will yeh tek me back ter Birnigum – Birmingham?' She chuckled at his slipping into the boater's dialect:

''Course we will, boy, if that's what yeh wants. After that – well, we'll see. Oi'll talk ter Mister Forrester, see if 'e can do anythin' ter get yeh out o' the mess yeh're in.'

'You'll do that fer me? Really?' She gave him a gentle shake:

'Oi'll do anythin' Oi can fer you, boy. Oi've still got a little girl, thanks ter you.'

They fell silent again, and relief washed over Jesse, threatening to bring tears to his eyes again. After a while, he lifted his head from her shoulder:

'Why were the cops waitin' back there? Did they know I was with yeh?'

'Someone saw yeh, at the Port. Yeh're famous, back there, boy, after what yeh did! The tale got to the coppers some'ow, 'n they put two 'n two tergether – there ain't many black kids on the boats! But they weren't sure, 'n Luke told 'em we'd left yeh there, s'far from Birnigum as yeh could get. They've gone back ter try 'n foind yeh, but Oi don' think they'll be tryin' too 'ard.' She paused: ''Round Birnigum'll be diff'rent, though, they'll still want yeh fer tekin' that money. But loike Oi says, Oi'll see what Mister Forrester can do 'bout it.'

'D'yeh think 'e'll be able ter 'elp me?'

'Loike as not, boy. Big man, 'e is! 'E's Mister Forrester Clayton, roight? 'E owns the coomp'ny.'

'Oh! Right...' But Jesse couldn't help harbouring doubts that such an important man wouldn't have time for someone like him. In the past, even his teachers hadn't had any time for him, leaving him to survive the tender mercies of his classmates on his own, so why would someone like Mr Clayton bother with him?

They sat in silence again, enjoying the quiet of the spring night. The comforting bulk of the boatwoman at his side gave Jesse the conviction that everything would be all right, if only he trusted her to help him. He drifted into daydreams of his own mother, of being held like this in her arms when he was just a little kid, how safe and secure it had felt...

Voices and raucous laughter sounded along the towpath, and a pair of dark figures staggered towards them, to stop, swaying gently, in front of them:

''Ello, Mam!'

'Luke! Oh, Luke, look at the state o' yeh!'

'H'I'm sorry, Annie – Oi think 'e's 'ad a bit too mooch...'

'Oi should think yeh are sorry, 'Arold Clutton! Look what yeh've done ter my boy!' Harold mumbled another apology and hurried away to his own boats, leaving Luke to fold unsteadily into a sitting position beside his mother:

'Shorry, Mam – they kep' on buyin' me pintsh o' ale 'n mekin' me drink 'em...'

''Ow can anyone *mek* yeh drink anythin', eh? Oh, Luke! Get off ter bed fer 'Eaven's sake. Jesse, will yeh 'elp 'im, lad?'

''Course, Missus Kain.' He stood up and helped the older boy to his feet, and together they staggered to the front of the boat to the sound of her muttered 'Stupid boy!' behind them.

'They shaid, if Oi were ter be a proper cap'n, Oi ortta be ebble ter tek me beer. Wadda you think, Jeshe?' Jesse helped him up onto the fore-deck, and down the steps into the tiny cabin. Luke's bed was still folded down from the morning, his mattress in place, and Jesse sat him on the edge of it, helped him struggle out of his coat and then bent down to pull off his boots. Not prepared to go any farther, he lifted his feet up onto the bed as Luke lay down, snuggling into a ball, his head on the pillow. As he began to snore, Jesse looked down at him:

'Jus' like my ol' man when 'e's 'ad a few! Sleep tight, Luke – 'n I don' fancy yer 'eadache in the mornin'!'

He undressed himself, to his vest and pants, and climbed into his own narrow bed. Wriggling under the rough blanket, he was almost drifting off to sleep as he heard mumbled from the far corner:

'Yeh know, mebbe yeh ain' shuch a bad kid, even if yeh ain' a boatee...'

Chapter Nineteen

'Unnh!' Jesse stirred and turned over on his tiny bed.

'O-oh...!' He pulled the blanket over his head, tried to settle again.

'Nnnh...' He gave up the unequal struggle and sat up, rubbing his eyes.

'Ooooh...' He looked over at the lumpy figue on the cross-bed, somewhere between annoyed and amused. The sounds of the older boy's distress weren't going to let him get any more sleep, but he couldn't help feeling sorry for him. He'd witnessed his father's rueful contemplation of a hangover more than once, and had an idea of what Luke was suffering: *Serves yeh right, yeh silly beggar!*

Grey light was filtering in through the porthole by his head; he pushed the blanket aside and groped for his shirt and trousers, pulled his boots and coat on and slid the hatch back. Smoke was already curling from the chimney of the aft cabin, telling him that a welcome mug of hot tea would be waiting for him. He climbed out, closing the hatch behind him, and walked the length of the deck, over the cabin and sat in the stern well; the doors opened and a hand appeared with two mugs of tea. He chuckled:

'Thank yeh! I don' think yeh'll be seein' Luke fer a while, though.' Mrs Kain's head followed the hand:

''Ow bad is 'e?'

'Pretty rough from the sound of 'im!' Jesse couldn't keep the amusement from his voice, and the boatwoman gave him a grin:

'Oi 'opes this'll teach 'im! 'E ain't never been drunk before. 'Is Pa'd slip 'im the odd 'alf a shandy now 'n agen, but 'e ain't never 'ad a skinful. Oi 'opes 'e'll learn!' Jesse laughed:

'It sounds like a pretty painful lesson!'

'Ah, well! But we needs 'im wi' the locks ter pass. 'Leven more 'ere 'n foive at Adderley, foive more t'other soide o' Drayton – 'n 'Ampton twenny-oone ternoight. Oi wants ter be oop there 'fore we stops, terday.'

'I can do 'em, Missus Kain.' She looked at him, doubtful:

'You go 'n roust 'im out, lad, get 'im movin'.' But Jesse shook his head:

'I really don' think 'e's up ter doin' anythin' this mornin'. My Dad's no use ter no-one if 'e's got a 'angover.' She remained unconvinced; he went on: 'I can manage! I knows what ter do now, I'll set 'em ahead for yeh, 'n you 'n the girls can get the boat through, right? It'd only be like you usually do, but wi' me instead o' Luke!' She still regarded him doubtfully, but at last gave in:

'All roight! Let the silly sod sleep then!' She turned to address her daughters, inside the cabin: 'Alice – Rosie – go 'n fetch the 'orse. You' she turned back to Jesse: 'grab a bit o' cheese ter nibble 'n go set the first'n.'

'Yes, Missus Kain!' Delighted at her trust in him, he leapt from the boat and hurried to fetch his windlass from the fore-cabin. Luke was now snoring noisily, huddled shapelessly under his blanket, and Jesse was grinning as he walked along the towpath to the nearby lock.

He was in luck. The last boats to pass the flight had come down the night before, leaving the locks all set ready for them, the bottom gates standing open in welcome. Jesse only had to close the paddle on his side, and then cross to the other to close that one: He'd seen Luke, and other boatmen, jump the gap between the footboards attached to the gates, at least six feet apart and high above the dark, cold water – dare he try the same trick to save him walking all the way around the lock? He tucked the windlass back into his belt and jumped, one foot in front of the other: *Yeah! That ain't so bad...*

He dropped the other paddle, and waited to close the gate. In his eagerness, he was much too early; Rosie was only just leading Prince up from the village, decked out in his ornate harness. He watched as she uncoiled the towrope and attached it to the spreader behind his back legs, and Alice walked up to be ready with the other gate. She looked over at him, concern in her eyes:

'No sign o' Luke, then?' He laughed:

'Nah! 'E's got a granddaddy of a 'angover, I reckon!'

'Stupid beggar!' Alice looked really angry: ''E knows we got ter get ahead terday!'

'Oh, we'll manage' Jesse reassured her: 'I'll do 'is bit, 'til 'e feels up ter it.'

'Oh Jesse...' The look in her eyes made his heart sing, but he just smiled at her.

Prince plodded past as Alice stepped back to avoid the towrope; the boat floated into the lock with Rosie at the helm, stopped neatly in place by a surge of water let in by Mrs Kain from a top paddle as they closed the two bottom gates behind it. She wound her paddle fully up, and quickly crossed to raise the other; Jesse and Alice hurried on the the next lock, to drop the raised bottom paddles and stand by the gates. In moments, the boatwoman was walking backwards, her bottom against the balance beam of the single top gate, swinging it open; a cluck from her lips set the horse in motion, and they repeated the whole exercise once again.

Then again. And again. And again, and again, up the close-set nine locks, then the last two of the flight, a little further apart. Barely an hour had passed, but they were well on their way, now travelling the mile-and-a-half pound to the five locks of Adderley, gratefully drinking the mugs of hot soup resurrected from the liquor of last night's stew and munching on crusty bread.

Working in the same pattern, they were soon up another thirty-one feet, through Adderley locks, and on the level stretch through Market Drayton.

Jesse was feeling pleased with himself; he felt they'd made just as quick progress as if Luke had been working with him – and he wasn't the only happy one. Rosie had a big grin on her face as she whispered to him:

'Mam's let me steer inter the locks terday!'

'H'only as long as yeh keeps yer moind on the job 'n yer eyes on where yeh're goin'!' her mother reminded her. 'Oi thought as Oi'd be best on the bank wi' you fer now' she told Jesse; and chuckled at the deflated look on his face: 'Yeh're doin' joost foine, boy! It's only 'cos yeh ain't got the h'experience what Luke's got, in case summat goes wrong.'

'I wonder 'ow 'e's feelin' now?' the boy speculated; Mrs Kain chuckled again:

'We'd best foind out! Rosie, tek 'im a mug o' tea, will yeh?'

Minutes later, Luke emerged to stand in the hatches of the fore-cabin. Even at that distance, Jesse could see that the other boy looked very pale, and his movements were slow and careful. Rosie sat talking to him for a while before coming back to join them:

''E says 'e ain't feelin' so bad now. But 'e still looks 'orrible!'

'Serve 'im roight! Go 'n tell 'im 'e's got 'alf an hour ter Tyrley locks. 'E can walk wi' the 'orse after that, 'elp clear 'is 'ead.'

She was soon back again, giggling fit to bust:

''E didn' know where we was! "'Ow'd we get 'ere?" 'e wanted ter know, so Oi told 'im it were thanks ter Jesse doin' 'is job fer 'im!'

Oh no! The last thing Jesse wanted was anything that might strain what he felt was an improving relationship with the older boy.

They passed by the town, and were soon at the bottom of the next flight. Luke had climbed from his cabin and joined them at the stern, and now he rose to the challenge of getting to work, setting the locks alongside Jesse. And it was perhaps just as well, because they now found a bad road before them, the locks set against them by boats travelling in the same direction. The boys worked together in a silence which owed more to Luke's physical condition than to any animosity between them, and they were soon through and on the seventeen-mile pound which would take them to the single lock of Wheaton Aston.

Luke, as instructed, set off at the heels of the horse, but he looked around in surprise as Jesse joined him.

'I fancy walkin' fer a bit – if yeh don' mind?' Luke shrugged:

'Suit yerself.'

''Ow're yeh feelin' now?'

'Oi'll do.'

Silence fell again. Very soon, the canal sank into the long, dark cutting at Woodseaves, and they were forced to walk in single file, squelching through the muddy puddles of the towpath; but before too long they rose into the daylight once more. Jesse ventured a question, something he'd been wondering about:

'D'yeh remember last night?'

''Ow d'yeh mean?'

'When yeh come back ter the boat?'

'Yeah – sort'a.'

'When yeh went ter bed?' Luke turned to him, and for once there was a grin on his face:

'Yeah, all roight! Yeh put me ter bed, didn't yeh? Thank yeh fer that.' He hesitated: 'Oi 'opes Oi didn' keep yeh awake?'

'Nah! Yeh did snore a bit, but it weren't too bad. But – after yeh was in bed? Yeh remember what yeh said ter me?' Luke looked blank, and shook his head:

'No – what did Oi say?' Jesse felt crestfallen:

'Oh – nothin'. It don' matter.'

The silence returned for a while, before Luke looked around:

'Listen- thank yeh fer gettin' oos ahead, terday. Kep' me out o' a lot o' trouble wi' Mam, that 'as.'

'That's okay. I enjoyed it – I enjoy workin' wi' the boat, with all o' yeh. I'm goin' ter miss it, when we gets back ter Birmingham.'

'Ah.'

Not long after, they were called back to the boat for dinner. Alice took over trudging behind Prince, and Jesse eagerly wolfed down his meal. Luke, however, picked at his food, forcing down as much as he could take, his face taking on an oddly greenish tinge:

'Sorry, Mam, Oi can' eat no more.' He pushed his plate away.

'All roight boy. Yeh can 'ave some more later, mebbe.'

'Yeah. Thanks, Mam.'

'D'yeh want ter lie down fer a bit? It's a way ter Wheaton yet.'

'Nah – Oi'll go walk wi' the 'orse agen. Fresh air'll do me good.' He stood up and went to step over the gunwale as his mother steered in against the bank. Jesse rose too, but Luke turned and put a restraining hand on his arm: 'No – Oi'm better on me own fer now, roight?'

'Oh – okay.' Jesse had thought to try and talk, build up a better rapport with him, and he felt upset at the boy's words. But Mrs Kain clapped him on the back as Luke strode away:

'Let 'im get over it, lad! 'E still looks pretty rough, don' 'e? 'N Oi reckon 'e's h'embarrassed, 'n all! 'E knows it's only 'cos you got stoock in that we're as far a'ead as this.'

Jesse gave her a smile and relaxed, sitting on the gunwale beside her. At the next bridge, Alice rejoined them and Mrs Kain stepped down into the cabin.

'Yeh goin' ter 'ave anoother go steerin' then?'

'Can I?'

''Course!' Alice stood aside, and he took the tiller again, pleased and proud. Rosie joined them in the afternoon sunshine, and the time passed easily as they chatted, comparing Jesse's life 'on the bank' with their own. Just past the town of Gnosall, they travelled through the short tunnel again, Luke this time walking in the dark with the horse while Alice took the tiller from Jesse with an apologetic smile. Once beyond it, he and Rosie took over on the towpath, walking with Prince for the last five miles to the next lock. Beyond Wheaton Aston, another two hours saw them at the shallow stop-lock by the canal junction – and the hard work of the Wolverhampton flight began again.

Once more working ahead with Luke, Jesse found himself again really enjoying the steady rhythm of walking on, draining down the next lock, opening the paired bottom gates and walking on again. They worked in silence, but now he didn't feel the old animosity radiating from his companion – it was rather that, knowing what they needed to do, words were not required. Behind them, Mrs Kain and the girls kept pace bringing the boat along.

Dusk gathered as they travelled, and it was full dark when they finally reached the top. A space on the towpath allowed them to tie up for the night just beyond the basin entrance on their left, and they gathered around the stern:

'Oi'm glad ter be 'ere!' Mrs Kain heaved a sigh of relief: 'We'll be h'empty by lunchtoime termorrer, then back ter the yard.' Her words left an empty feeling in Jesse's stomach, knowing that he'd then be leaving them, but she turned to him with a smile: 'Yeh've been a great 'elp terday, Jesse, we wouldn' be 'ere without yeh.' Luke groaned:

'There's no need ter rub it in, Mam!' She laughed:

'Serve yeh roight, boy! 'Ow're yeh feelin' now?'

'Ruddy 'ungry!'

'Oi reckons we deserves a treat – 'ow 'bout some fish 'n chips fer supper?' She laughed again at the chorus of assent: 'Roight then! Luke, you 'n Jesse go fer 'em, there's a good little chippy a coupl'a streets away.' She counted out her last few coins, and the two boys set off while the girls led Prince away to the stables.

Chapter Twenty

They found the fish and chip shop with no difficulty, a small group of local youths standing outside, smoking and talking. Luke handed the money over to Jesse:

''Ere, you go 'n get 'em. Coupl'a bits o' fish, 'n plenty o' chips, roight?'

'Ain't you comin' in?'

'Nah...' Luke hesitated: 'You can read what it says on the board, roight? Oi med a fool o' meself once, askin' fer summat they 'adn' got.'

'Oh – okay then.' He left the older boy outside and went into the hot, oily atmosphere inside the shop. He waited while a mother and her little girl were served, and then stepped up to the counter:

'Two small cod 'n 'six pen'orth o' chips, please.' He could feel his own tummy rumbling in anticipation as he watched the fish being wrapped in sheets of old newspaper and placed on top of the huge pile of chips. The package duly wrapped, he handed over Mrs Kain's money and took the proffered change.

Outside the shop, Luke lounged against the wall beside the doorway. The group of youths split up, several of them walking away; three remained, and the one who appeared to be the ring-leader looked at the boat boy:

'Hey.' Luke looked up:

'Yeah?'

'You ain't from round 'ere, are yeh?'

'No.'

'Where're yeh from then?'

'Joost travellin' through, loike.'

'I didn' ask that – I said where're yeh from?' Luke just shrugged, not interested in striking up a conversation, but the youth wouldn't let it go:

'Come on, give! This is ar territ'ry, roight? What're yeh doin' 'ere?'

'Oi tol' yeh, we ain't stoppin', 'cept fer ternoight.' There was an eagerness in the youth's voice now:

'Yeh're a boatee, ain't yeh? A dirty boatee!' Luke bridled, but he kept his temper:

'So what if Oi am, then?'

'We don' loike yer koind 'round 'ere, that's what.' The other two joined in now:

'Yeah, dirty boatee!'

'Let's teach 'im a lesson!'

The ring-leader grabbed the lapels of his coat and dragged him away from the wall, and all three set to, punching and kicking. Luke fought back as best he could, but three onto one didn't give him much hope – and they were all bigger than him.

Jesse emerged from the shop at that moment, and stopped, aghast at what was happening. After suffering so many years of bullying, he knew how to look after himself – but these were three lads, older and bigger than either him or Luke. He looked around for a weapon, but nothing came to hand. That wasn't going to stop him, but he knew they were not going to get away lightly; he dropped the bundle of fish and chips and went to throw himself into the fight – but then he realised: he'd forgotten the windlass again, and it was still stuck in the back of his belt! A surge of glee ran through him - that might even the odds a bit...

He grabbed it out, and, whirling it over his head, ran at the youths attacking Luke. One turned to fend him off, only to get the windlass cracked hard against his arm; he bent over with a yell, holding his injury, and Jesse brought it down on his exposed head with a dull thud. The youth reeled away, and he swung at the next bully, hitting him hard on the shoulder. The youth turned around, surprised and hurt:

'Hey! That ain't fair!'

'So three onter one's fair, is it?' Jesse snarled at him, and swung the windlass again. The youth ducked, and threw a punch; Jesse leant back out of the way and brought the windlass down hard on his exposed neck. The youth swore loudly and swung again, only to receive a painful blow as his hand met the swinging windlass.

Luke, heartened by Jesse's support, drove his paired fists into the last bully's stomach; Jesse's opponent lashed out with a foot but went sprawling as his lithe assailant dodged clear. Scrambling to his feet, he turned to run; Luke gave the last one a hearty kick on the shin as he too fled.

They stood looking at each other, and then burst into laughter:

'We saw 'em off, didn' we?' Luke was grinning from ear to ear.

'Yeah! Right 'n proper, we did!' Jesse's grin was just as wide.

'That'll teach 'em ter call oos dirty boatees, eh?'

'Yeah!' And then Luke's words registered in Jesse's mind: 'What?'

'What?'

'You said – 'us'.' Luke stared at him for a moment; then he grinned:

'Yeah, well. You ain't one o' them, are yeh?'

The mood was broken as the door beside them opened:

'Hey, boys?' They turned to the fish-shop owner: 'Are you two all roight?' They both ran their hands over their arms and bodies:

'Yeah, reckon so.'

'Bit bruised mebbe!' Luke was still grinning.

'What about yer fish?' Jesse looked down – the package he'd dropped had got kicked and trodden on in the melee:

'Oh no! Oh 'Ell...' But the man took his arm:

'You coom back in lad. Yeh're together, are yeh, you two?'

'Yeah, that's right.'

'Well, them three's been makin' no end of a nuisance o' themselves 'round 'ere. You ain't goin' without yer supper on account o' them.' And he gave them two fresh pieces of fish, and an even bigger pile of chips, and waved them on their way with a cheery: 'Don' ferget where me shop is now, yeh hear?'

They headed back to the boat, still buoyed up by their triumph over the local toughs. Jesse carried the new bundle of food; as they turned the corner at the end of the road, Luke said:

'Hey – thank yeh, fer what yeh did back there. Oi'd've got a roight beatin' if yeh 'adn' stepped in.' Jesse shrugged:

'S'okay. I've got beaten enough, at school 'n that.'

'Yeah... But yeh could've joost left me to it – Oi mean...'

'Like you could've 'anded me in ter the cops, more'n once?'

'Yeah, roight... Listen – Oi knows Oi've been 'ard on yeh, roight? 'N, well, mebbe Oi was wrong, roight? What Oi'm troyin' ter say is, well, Oi'm sorry, h'okay?' Jesse looked around, surprised but so pleased:

'Tha's okay, Luke. I never meant ter be no trouble ter yeh...'

'You ain't been, not really. It's joost – Oi ain't used ter 'avin' no-one else around, loike. We might even mek a boatee out o' yeh yet!' A grin spread across Luke's face, to be echoed by the one on Jesse's:

'Yeh reckon?' His heart was soaring now.

'Yeh did a real good job terday – loike Mam said, we wouldn'a got 'ere if it weren' fer you.' And Luke's arm was around his shoulders: 'Yeh ain't a bad kid at all – even if yeh are a foonny colour!'

Jesse burst out laughing, getting a startled chuckle from Luke – after so many years of being put down because of the colour of his skin, to have it turned into a joke seemed like the most wonderful thing that could happen. For once, he felt that he was accepted for the person he was, not seen just as 'that black kid', and the lightness in his heart was beyond belief.

Mrs Kain looked up as the two boys walked along the towpath, back from the town, and stared, unbelieving, at the sight of her son with his arm around the brown boy's shoulders, the two of them chuckling together. Jesse handed over the fish and chips with the grin still on his face, and they all sat around the stern well, tucking into the communal pile.

'So what's got you two so cheerful, all of a sudden?' she asked.

'Oh, we 'ad a bit of a run-in wi' some o' the locals' Jesse told her.

'Yeah' Luke confirmed: 'Three of 'em. Called me a dirty boatee, 'n troyed ter beat me oop – but Jesse 'ere coom out o' the shop 'n weighed in. We sent 'em packin', didn' we?' Jesse laughed:

'We did 'n all!'

They rounded the meal off in a mood of celebration when Alice remembered the bars of chocolate waiting for them, in the little cupboard under the cabin steps where they stored their milk and meat to keep cool.

Chapter Twenty-One

The mood in the fore-cabin when the boys awoke the next morning was positively jovial. Jesse stayed under his blanket, leaving the cramped space free for Luke to dress first – but the older boy gave a groan as he swung his legs out of bed:

'Oh 'Ell! Look, me knee's got all swole oop durin' the noight.'

'What's the cause o' that, d'yeh reckon?'

'Oi took a kick on it las' noight, but it didn' 'urt then. Ruddy-well does now, though!'

'You better tek it easy terday then.'

'Ah, reckon so.' He pulled on his clothes and left the cabin while Jesse got dressed. Soon the two of them were draining mugs of tea and munching on bread and butter while the girls went to collect Prince from the stables. Mrs Kain had tut-tutted over Luke's knee:

'Yeh will get in these silly foights! Yeh'd best steer terday, troy 'n rest it.'

'We didn' start it, Mam!'

'That's right, it was them other fellas!' Jesse sprang to his defence, and she laughed:

'It's good ter see you two on the same soide, any'ow! Yeh've got it easy fer a bit, there's no locks now 'til we turns oop the Crow' she told Jesse.

''Ow far's that?'

''Bout three hours' Luke answered him.

It slowly turned into another delightful spring day, the early mist clearing as the sun rose over the drab dark buildings of Wolverhampton. Alice and Rosie walked together behind the horse, and Mrs Kain bustled quietly about in the cabin, tidying up and beginning to prepare a dinner for later; Jesse climbed up to sit on the side of the cabin roof as Luke leant on the tiller, and the two boys sank deep into conversation. Jesse found himself repeating much of what he'd already told the girls, about his life on the bank, in London, and then about what had happened since his move to Birmingham. He found Luke's perspective of life on the canal fascinating, as the one who was at least nominally in charge of the boat, and listened eagerly to the boy's tales of mishap and adventure on the water, taking delight in the misfortunes of others as only boys together can.

They followed the meandering course of the old Birmingham Canal, Jesse watching the changing scenery, housing estates occasionally interrupting the largely industrial landscape around them. This was the stretch he'd missed before, catching up on his sleep in the cabin after that dreadful night under the railway bridge. But thoughts of that only reminded him that they would very soon now be at their journey's end, and he felt a growing sorrow at the thought of leaving them, especially now that he and Luke were on friendly terms. And the prospect of having to try and make his own way, in a strange city, did nothing to bolster his mood – although, if the boatwoman's promise came true, he might at least no longer have to fear the police looking for him and returning him to that awful foster-home...

They crossed a number of canal junctions, surprising Jesse that there was so much of a network of waterways. Luke chuckled:

'They says as there's more canals in Birnigum than there is in Venice. That's a town in h'Italy what's famous fer its canals. S'what Mister Forrester says, any'ow.'

Another junction, and this time they took a right-hand turn, past a narrow lock; soon after, and they turned left again. And then suddenly Jesse knew where he was – a massive iron railway bridge loomed in front of them:

'Is this...?'

'Yeah – this's where we found yeh!'

A mile on, and Jesse was dumbfounded to look over the parapet of an aqueduct to find himself looking down upon another canal. His expression got Luke laughing again:

'Tol' yeh there was lots o' cuts 'round 'ere! Look t'other way, 'n yeh'll see where it goes under the 'ill.' Jesse did so, and true enough, the lower canal vanished into the darkness only yards away from where they floated past.

It was still only mid-morning when Luke pointed across the canal:

'There y'are – that's 'ome!'

''Ome?' I didn' think yeh 'ad one?'

'Nearest thing we got! Tha's Clayton's yard, we'll be stoppin' in there later, once we're empt.' Several other boats were tied at the side, and Jesse saw that they all bore the same colours as their own. One was drawn up on the bank, with a timber shed apparently over one end, and the sound of men at work drifted out to his ears.

They passed the yard, under a bridge, and Luke nudged him:

'Watch this mate!' Another bridge, an open iron structure on brick piers, spanned the water in front of them, and just beyond a branch canal turned off to their right. Alice led the horse underneath and along the side of the ramp which clearly led back up onto the bridge itself. At the end of the ramp, she turned Prince and led him up the slope; the towline fell slack as horse and boat approached each other, and then Prince turned across the bridge. Luke was heaving the tiller, swinging the boat's fore-end around the corner which lay beyond; and then Prince descended from the bridge again onto the towpath of the branch canal, and the rope drew tight again. And now, before them lay a lock.

Jesse picked up the windlass which he'd laid ready on the cabin-top as Mrs Kain emerged from within. Luke reached for his windlass, but Jesse took his arm:

'I'll do these – you stay there 'n rest yer knee.'

'Yeh sure?'

''E's roight Luke, you stay where y'are' the boatwoman told her son. He knew better than to argue:

'H'okay Mam!' The boys exchanged grins as Jesse stepped over the side onto the towpath. The locks were against them, and he hurried to close the top gate and draw the first one off. *These're easy!* Instead of the paired bottom gates, these had only a single gate, making his life that much simpler, and in moments he had it swinging open ready for the boat.

In no time at all, it seemed, they had cleared all six locks, working together with only the occasional word, each knowing what the others would do, in an easy rhythm. Jesse stepped back onto the deck as Alice clucked Prince into motion, and Mrs Kain gave him a smile:

'T'ain't far now! Joost past the railway 'n we're there.'

The canal led them around a bend, under the arch of the railway bridge, and then a huge brick-built warehouse loomed on their left. And just beyond lay their destination: Alice detached the towrope from Prince's harness and stood ready to pass it on board; at Luke's instruction, Jesse ran forward to take it from her and coil it on the fore-deck. The boat was swinging the other way across the channel now, its momentum carrying it along until the fore-end nudged the bank just where a strange-looking contraption of derricks and hoses stood, apparently unattended. As the bow grated against wooden piles set into the canal-side, two men emerged from a little white-painted building. One took the fore-end mooring line from Jesse, and the other hurried to the stern to catch that rope as Luke threw it.

Greetings were exchanged, but with little else said the hoses were soon swung out. Luke and Jesse lifted the hatches in the boat's deck, and the hoses were lowered in; pumps started, and in minutes the boat began to ride higher in the water. One of the men rolled an obviously-heavy barrel across the wharf, and Jesse, remembering Luke's painful knee, helped him to shift it onto the boat where they stood it right over to one side:

'What's that fer?' he asked.

'You ain't done this before, 'ave yeh?' He shook his head, and the man laughed: 'We uses that ter mek the boat tilt over ter the soide. That way we can get pretty mooch all o' the oil out, see?'

And true enough, as the load was emptied, the boat took on more and more of a tilt. The men wrestled the hoses into the lowest corner of the holds, and soon the slurping noises from within told them that the oil was all removed into the big cylindrical tanks on the wharfside. The wharf foreman had been chatting with Mrs Kain while the unloading was going on; now he turned away with a cheerful:

'Thanks! See yeh nex' toime, eh?'

They rolled the barrel off and away, making the *Murray* lurch back upright, now riding high out of the water as it had been when Jesse first saw it. Luke took the long shaft from the deck as Jesse untied the ropes, and poled the fore-end across the canal; as it drifted closer, he coiled the tow-rope in his hand and threw it to where Alice stood patiently waiting. She hooked it onto the harness once more, and they were away, still heading further up the branch canal, Mrs Kain at the tiller.

Under another bridge, and just approaching a second, Alice stopped to unhook the tow again. A wide basin here allowed enough room for the seventy-foot-long boat to be turned around; Luke once more set to with the shaft, driving the bow around in one direction as his mother rowed the tiller in the other. Slowly, the empty boat turned, and soon Jesse was able to pass the towrope back to Alice once again.

Now, they were heading back, past the oil wharf, past the warehouse, under the railway bridge and back to the locks.

Dropping as quickly down as they had worked up them earlier, it was still barely lunchtime when they tied the boat at the side of the company's yard. Alice led Prince over the nearby bridge and took him to the stables to rest and feed, while Luke and Jesse set about giving the boat a good mopping-down. Mrs Kain brewed a fresh pot of tea; Rosie had spotted friends from another of the boats, and ran off to play.

Wielding his mop, Jesse's spirits sank – this was the end of his holiday, the break that Mrs Kain had promised him. Now, he was back on his own resources, in charge of his own destiny, and the prospect left him sad and depressed. But the last week had shown him that he could make a go of a new situation – so maybe it wouldn't be so bad, after all. He'd survive. He'd have to!

Chapter Twenty-Two

As they mopped and cleaned, some of the other boaters came over to talk, and Jesse found himself quietly accepted as one of their number, even if he was also aware of a kind of surreptitious curiosity directed at him. And then a tall, broad-shouldered fellow strolled over, and Luke looked up:

''Ello, Mister Dulson! 'Ow are yeh?'

'We're foine, Luke. 'Ow's yer Mam? 'N little Rosie, Oi 'eard as she took a look oop at the Port?'

'They're h'okay, thanks. Rosie's foine – Jesse 'ere fished 'er out!'

'Ah – so Oi 'eard. Well done, young fella!' Jesse shook the proffered hand, rather nervous of the man's congratulation.

Dulson turned back to Luke: 'Mister Forrester's 'ere from Bren'ford, in the h'office – 'e said as 'e wanted a word wi' yeh when yeh got 'ere.'

'Oh, roight! Oi'd better go 'n see 'im then.' Luke dropped his mop and walked away, still limping slightly from his damaged knee.

Minutes later, he was back, accompanied by a man of about sixty, well-dressed in a tweed jacket with a smart trilby hat. Mrs Kain emerged from the cabin as they approached, a smile on her homely face:

''Ello, Mister Forrester. It's good ter see yeh.'

'Hello, Ann. How are you all?'

'We're foine, thank yeh. Sorry we're a bit late, this trip – we got 'eld oop a bit.' The man chuckled:

'Yes, I heard! I'm so glad that little Rosie is safe – how is she after her terrible experience?'

'She's foine, thank yeh – she's off playin' wi' the other kiddies.'

'That's good!' The man turned to Jesse: 'And you must be Mrs Kain's extra hand? I understand we owe Rosie's life to you, young man.' He held out his hand, and Jesse took it nervously, rather awe-struck by the familiarity of such an important man. Forrester Clayton smiled at him: 'Well done!'

'Thank yeh, sir.'

'Mister Forrester?' Mrs Kain spoke up: 'Oi was goin' ter ask yeh, if mebbe yeh could do summat ter 'elp young Jesse 'ere. Yeh see...' The man held up his hand, smiling still:

'I know all about this young fellow! After I heard he was with you, and about what he did, I made it my business to find out.' He turned back to Jesse: 'So – what are we going to do about you, Mister Carter?' Jesse hung his head:

'I don' know, sir. I'd be very grateful fer any 'elp yeh can offer me. I'm in a bit of a spot...'

'I know all about your troubles, too!' Clayton interrupted him, chuckling again: 'Now – how much was it you took from your foster-parents?'

'Two poun' ten shillin's, sir.' Jesse's eyes were still on his boots, but he looked up in surprise as Clayton said:

'Well, we can soon deal with that! I'm prepared to return that money, with maybe a little extra to encourage them, shall we say, to drop all charges against you?' Jesse didn't know what to say:

'I... That would be... I'll pay yeh back, I promise, some'ow...' Clayton chuckled again:

'You will indeed, young man! How much do you have left of it?'

'One poun' eighteen 'n fourpence, sir.' He stuck a hand in his pocket and withdrew the handful of notes and coins: ''Ere yeh are, Mister Clayton.' The man took it from him:

'Very good – so you owe me eleven shillings and eightpence?'

'Yes, sir.'

'All right, we'll worry about that later. But if we settle this matter it will give you a chance to start again, eh?'

'Yes sir! Thank you, sir.'

'But that still leaves the question of what you are going to do, doesn't it?'

'Yes sir.'

'And where you're going to live. Oh well, we'll come to that in a minute. In the meantime, Ann, Luke, I need to talk to you about your boat. We've had a letter from the health inspectors at Ellesmere Port – they're not happy about that cracked flue on the fore-cabin stove, and there are a few other issues.' He held up a hand as Mrs Kain went to speak: 'You know and I know that you won't be using that stove until the winter comes again, but these are government officials, and you can't expect them to have the necessary common-sense to understand that. They really are most insistent that we should fix it right away. And it doesn't make sense to hold the boat up unless we give it a full docking, so we are going to slip the *Murray* the day after tomorrow, when the *Tove* goes back in the water. It means a days delay, but you can take that boat over.'

'But Mister Forrester...'

'The *Tove* ain't got no fore-cabin!' Luke, interrupting, was clearly puzzled: ''Ow're we goin' ter manage?' Clayton's hands were up again, pacifying them:

'I know, I know! With Luke here being sixteen now' A sly wink at the boy told them that he knew all about Luke's exaggerated age as well: 'you have to have two cabins. But if you had two *boats...*' They began to protest again, but he hushed them once more:

'You know very well that the company wants to introduce more motor boats on the oil contract. It means quicker deliveries, and more tonnage carried each trip. With a motor and butty, you could be carrying forty-five tons and still turning around in a week – and that means earning nearly twice as much money. Doesn't that sound attractive to you?'

'Well, yeah, but – there's only the four of oos, 'n two o' them's young girls...' Luke sounded doubtful; his mother was eyeing Jesse, her own expression more thoughtful. Clayton went on:

'Whatever the politicians say, there's a war coming. Mr Chamberlain is deluding himself if he thinks otherwise, I'm quite certain, and when it comes, the oil traffic will be even more important than it is now. So I will be very happy if I can get your crew running a pair of boats, sooner rather than later, Luke. What do you say?'

'Oi don' know...' Forrester Clayton wasn't going to give up:

'We've got a new boat, just being finished down at Uxbridge. A motor, with a Bolinder engine, brand new, called the *Swan,* after a river in Western Australia – It's yours, if you'll take it.'

Luke looked at his mother; she returned his gaze, a little smile crossing her face, and then turned to Clayton:

'Loike Luke says, it'd be 'ard work in them narrer locks on the Shroppie cut, wi' joost 'im 'n me 'n the girls. But if we 'ad anoother 'and...'

'Exactly.' They both looked at Jesse:

'Yeh said as yeh knows a bit 'bout injuns, didn' yeh?' Mrs Kain asked him; he nodded, caught between self-doubt and a surging excitement:

'Yeah – but that's motor-car engines, not boats! I s'pose I could learn, though...' His thoughts strayed back to the impressive big diesel he'd inspected at Ellesmere Port: 'I'd *like* ter learn more 'bout 'em!' Clayton was smiling, a satisfied look on his face:

'Well, I think that's settled then! I'm sure you won't mind having another mouth to feed, Ann, with all the extra money you'll be earning? And we don't need to worry about your future, at least for a while, Jesse?'

'Yes sir – I mean no sir...' Clayton turned to Luke:

'I'm driving back to London in the morning, to my office – if I drop the two of you at Uxbridge, I'm sure you could bring the *Swan* back here in a few days? We'll pay you for the trip, of course.' Luke and Jesse exchanged grins; Luke answered for both of them:

''Course we can, Mister Forrester!'

None of them spoke for a moment as Forrester Clayton turned and strode away, but every face carried the same happy grin.

'Jesse!' Alice had returned from the stables in time to overhear the end of the conversation – now she ran up and threw her arms around the brown boy's neck: 'Yeh're goin' ter stay with oos!'

'Looks like it!' He hugged her back, and felt her mother's hand on his shoulder. He looked at her:

'Will that suit yeh, lad?' He nodded eagerly:

'Not 'alf!' He let go of Alice and turned to Luke, who grinned at him:

'Oi've alwes wanted a brother 'stead o' joost bloomin' sisters! There's joost one thing?'

'What's that?' Jesse asked.

'D'yeh moind if Oi calls yeh Jess? Oi still can't get my 'ead 'round Jessie as a boy's name.'

A Few Words of Explanation!

Hello, Dear Reader.

I hope you've enjoyed my little story; I hope I have perhaps been able to take you back sixty years or so, into a world that doesn't exist any more. Oh, the canals are still there, or most of them; some of you might even have been out on them, on holiday in a hired boat perhaps, or walked along the towpath, or gone fishing in them. But the world of Annie Kain, and Luke and Alice and Rosie, the world that Jess stumbled into, is gone now.

Britain's canals were built, between the middle of the 1700s and around 1830, as the country's first 'motorways'. Don't laugh – that was how the people then saw them! Not for travelling around on themselves, perhaps, but as a super-quick, super-easy way of transporting goods around. Well, quick by comparison with the other ways they had then – the canals were there before the railways, when the only other way of moving anything was by horse and cart. I'm sure a lot of you knew that – I hope you'll forgive me for saying it again, but maybe some folk didn't know. And boats still carried cargoes on the canals, despite the arrival of the railways, until after the Second World War.

For most of the years in between, the people who worked on the boats, like the Kains, also lived on board, in the tiny back-cabins as I've tried to describe in the story. Some boats, like the *Murray,* had a small extra cabin at the front, but of course this took up a bit of the space that would otherwise hold more cargo, so the extra room came at a price – remember, the boatman only got paid for the weight of cargo he delivered! The boat people were a very private lot – they didn't, as a rule, get on too well with folks 'on the bank', and most people there thought that the boatees were not much better than gypsies. Not that there's anything wrong with gypsies, any more than there was with the boaters, as I hope you can tell! But that was how 'ordinary' people thought of them.

I'm not going to bore you with a lot of guff about history, or tell you how a lock works – if you don't know, you can easily find out for yourselves! (Isn't the internet wonderful?) But – and this is especially for those of you who have been boating on the canal, or might do so one day soon – I ought to explain a bit about the 'old-fashioned' way of working the boats. As Luke pointed out to Jess, time was money for the old boaters, so they did things in the quickest, most efficient way they could. Nowadays, when we're boating, we're usually on holiday, so we've got all the time in the world; and all of us are amateurs. The old boatmen always knew that the next folks along would be professionals, like them, and would know exactly what to do, and that meant they could, so to speak, 'cut corners' in the way they did things.

Nowadays, when we leave a lock, we are supposed to shut the gates and make sure all the paddles are closed too. But back then, they didn't do that! They would leave the gates standing open, and the paddles still raised, as they hurried on to the next lock. That's why, in the story, sometimes Luke and Jess had to close the far gates and fill (or empty) each lock, and sometimes (like when Luke had his hangover) they would find the locks all ready for them, with nothing to do. Mind you, they'd do it differently if they knew there was another boat, or a pair, following close behind – then, most of them would not only close the gates and paddles, but if it was someone they knew behind, they'd actually raise a paddle at the other end to start the lock getting ready for them.

Of course, you don't see horse-drawn boats on the canal these days. Well, almost never! Our boats have engines, and that means that you can put the engine in reverse, so that the propeller, going backwards, will stop the boat. But a horse boat doesn't have any brakes – that's why, coming into the locks when they were full, going downhill, Mrs Kain, or Alice, would what they called 'strap the boat in'. That meant using a heavy piece of rope (the strap) attached at the back of the boat, which they'd loop over a sort of protrusion on the end of the lock-gate as they floated past. As it pulled tight, it would snatch the gate shut behind them, and bring the boat to a stop at the same time. You can still do that, at least at some locks, but it's kind of disapproved of now – and we've got the engine, anyway! And going uphill, they'd stop the boat in the empty lock by opening a paddle at the top end, so the surge of water stopped it. That's not approved of nowadays, either!

Some of you might have heard about what they called 'legging'. That was the way the old boatmen would take a boat through most of the canal tunnels – usually, there was no towpath through the tunnels, so they had to get the boat through while the children led the horse over the top of the hill. It was done by the boatman and his wife, lying on boards attached to the front deck, literally walking along the walls of the tunnel. But on the Shropshire Union Canal, Rosie's 'little tunnel' at Gnosall in my story does have a towpath going right through, so they could just let the horse carry on pulling the boat. And the tunnel at Coseley, near Wolverhampton, which they went through as well, is the same. The 'big'un' at Harecastle, which she told Jess about, has no towpath, which is why she mentions the tug which would tow the boats, usually a bunch of them at once, right through, while she would have to take Prince over the top.

Jess's story is set in the spring of 1939, just before the Second World War began. I'm sure most of you will have worked that out, anyway! In case you were wondering, Thomas Clayton

(Oldbury) Ltd was a real company, that did run the sort of 'tanker' boats that I've described. And the oil run, from Stanlow in Cheshire all the way down the Shropshire Union Canal to Langley Green, near Oldbury, really did happen – it started in 1924, and went on all through the war and up to 1955. Most of the people in my story are fictitious, of course – but some of them aren't! Abel Beechey really did run the *Stour* and the *Hudson* (pretty well all the Clayton boats were named after rivers), and there really was a Mr Dulson. And Forrester Clayton was the managing director of the company from 1927 until his death in 1942.

If you ever get the chance, pay a visit to the National Waterways Museum at Ellesmere Port (yes, the same place as in the story). Not only will you be able to see what the canals are like there, where the Chester Canal meets the Manchester Ship Canal, but they've even got a restored Clayton's horse boat – with a fore-cabin, like the *Murray*. It's called the Gifford – take a good look, and you'll be able to envisage what life might have been like for Luke and Alice, and little Rosie.

And if you've enjoyed my little tale, you might want to know that I'm thinking about writing another. Perhaps telling how Luke and Jess got on, bringing the *Swan* back from Uxbridge...

Geoffrey Lewis
June 2010